A Whisper and a Wish

A Whisper and a Wish

ROBIN JONES GUNN

BETHANY HOUSE PUBLISHERS
MINNEAPOLIS, MINNESOTA 55438

A Whisper and a Wish
Revised edition 1998
Copyright © 1989, 1998
Robin Jones Gunn

Edited by Janet Kobobel
Cover illustration and design by the Lookout Design Group

Scripture quotations taken from *The Holy Bible, New International Version*
copyright © 1973, 1978, 1984 International Bible Society.

Focus on the Family books are available at special quantity discounts when
purchased in bulk by corporations, organizations, churches, or groups. Special
imprints, messages, and excerpts can be produced to meet your needs. For
more information, contact: Resource Sales Group, Focus on the Family, 8605
Explorer Drive, Colorado Springs, CO 80920; or phone (800) 932-9123.

A Focus on the Family book published by
Bethany House Publishers
A Ministry of Bethany Fellowship International
11400 Hampshire Avenue South
Bloomington, Minnesota 55438
www.bethanyhouse.com

Printed in the United States of America by
Bethany Press International, Bloomington, Minnesota 55438

Library of Congress Cataloging-in-Publication Data

Gunn, Robin Jones, 1955–
   A whisper and a wish / Robin Jones Gunn.
      p. cm. — (The Christy Miller series)
   Summary: When her family relocates to California, 15-year-old Christy
Miller faces new dreams and disappointments as she decides what price she's
willing to pay for making new friends.
   ISBN 1–56179–598–4
   [1. Friendship—Fiction. 2. Conduct of life—Fiction. 3. Moving,
household—Fiction.] I. Title. II. Series
PZ7.G972Wh   1989
[Fic]—dc20   89–23258
                                            CIP
                                            AC

02 03 04 05 06 07 08 09 / 19 18 17 16 15 14 13 12 11 10 9 8 7

Contents

CHAPTER ONE

Paula, My Friend

Tall, slim Christy Miller eagerly tapped on the front door of her best friend's house. "Come on, Paula, answer the door!" she mumbled, clenching the crumpled Disneyland shopping bag in her hand. Her denim shorts and bright yellow T-shirt, bought while in California, made her feel as though she were still on the beach, not back home in Wisconsin.

The door opened, and Christy shouted, "Surprise!"

But it was Paula's mom who stood behind the screen door. "Christy?" she said with some hesitation.

"Hi! Is Paula home?"

"Well, come in! I almost didn't recognize you, with your hair cut short. When did you get back?"

"Last night."

"I thought you were staying with your aunt and uncle until the end of the summer."

"I was, but my parents had me come home early so I could help with the move and everything."

Paula's mom shook her head. "We still can't believe your folks decided to sell the farm. Not that we blame them. It's been tough financially for all of us."

"Did they tell you we're moving to California?" Christy asked excitedly.

"Yes. Paula's already asked if she can stay with you next summer."

"Can she?"

"She's in her room. Why don't you go ask her?"

Christy slipped down the hallway, her heart pounding. She had been gone almost two months and had changed so much. Had Paula changed? Should she knock or walk in?

Christy chose the sneak approach. Slowly, she inched the door open. Paula sat on her bed with her back to the door and the radio on loud enough to cover Christy's footsteps as she tiptoed in. Sneaking up to the edge of the bed, Christy leaned over so her face was right against the back of Paula's head. "Boo!" she shouted.

Paula shrieked, fell off the bed, and knocked the phone off the nightstand.

"Christy!" she screamed, then jumped up, snatched a pillow off her bed, and heaved it at Christy. "Give me a heart attack, why don't you!"

Paula's long, straight blond hair fell in front of her face as she grabbed another pillow. An all-out pillow fight ensued until Paula shouted over Christy's laughter, "Wait a minute! Wait a minute!" She picked up her phone.

"Hello? Hello? Oh well," Paula said with a laugh, "I guess she'll call back."

The two friends flopped onto the bed, caught their breath, and looked each other over. Paula still had a baby-doll face and round, flushed cheeks. But something in her eyes made her seem older than when Christy had seen her last.

"Christy!" Paula squealed. "Look at you! You're so tan, and

your hair—I can't believe it! You said it was short, but it's so light. Did the sun do that?"

"I guess so. Or maybe it was the saltwater. I don't know. So? Did you miss me?"

"Did I miss you! Are you kidding! I can't believe how different you look." Suddenly, Paula's expression got serious. "Is it true your parents sold the farm and you're moving to California?"

"Yes!" Christy bubbled. "Isn't that too good to be true? When my parents called and said I had to come home early, I thought something terrible must have happened. I never dreamed they would tell me we were all moving to California!"

Paula tugged on the frayed edges of her cut-off shorts.

"Start saving your money for next summer, Paula, because when you come stay with me, we're going to have such a great time! I'll get my aunt to take us shopping, and we'll have barbecues on the beach with all my new friends, and Paula, you are going to love Todd. He's the most fantastic guy in the world!"

Paula smiled a still, polite smile.

Christy stopped. "What? What's wrong?"

"Nothing. Go on. You were saying how you're in love with Todd."

Christy giggled. "He gave me flowers, Paula! When I left yesterday, he surprised me with a big bouquet of white carnations, and then . . ." Christy paused. "Paula, what's wrong? Tell me."

"Well, it's just that you're leaving," Paula said with a sniffle, "and it doesn't seem to bother you a bit."

"What do you mean?" Christy slipped off her sandals and listened closely to her friend.

"All your letters from California this summer sounded so wonderful, bragging about all those exciting places you went to and all the stuff your aunt bought you—like all your dreams were coming true. And here I sat, day after day, bored out of my brain."

"But, Paula, it wasn't perfect like you think. Some really hard things happened this summer, too. It wasn't all fancy restaurants and adventures." Christy paused and remembered Shawn's death, all the times she felt she didn't belong, and the insecurities she experienced with Todd. "I had to grow up a lot."

"Still, Christy, you had a dream summer. Admit it! And now you're moving back there, and you don't even act sad about it."

"Well, I'm sad about leaving you, but you're going to come stay with me next summer. Can't you see why I'd be excited to move back there?"

"I guess, but still—"

The phone rang and Paula answered with a sulky "Hello."

"Oh, hi! It's you," she said brightly. "Yes, I'm sorry. My phone got knocked over. What? Really? Tonight? Yeah, I'm sure I can. Who? You're kidding! He's such a TWB! I'm definitely coming. I'd better go. There's somebody here. Okay. Bye."

Christy smiled but felt tense inside. *Who's on the phone that can make Paula change from glum to sunshine so instantly?*

"Who was that?" Christy asked

"Melissa. You don't know her. She works at Dairy Queen. Her brother is a TWB, if you know what I mean." Paula's blue eyes looked like the big, round eyes of a baby doll.

"No, I don't know what you mean." Christy tried to hide her hurt feelings.

"Oh," Paula said flippantly, "it's this little code Melissa and I made up. It stands for Total Whompin' Babe. He's going to be at Melissa's party tonight. Look, I've got a picture of him. Is he a TWB, or what?" She held out a photo of a tall guy dressed in a black leather jacket, standing next to a motorcycle, with his arms folded in front of him.

"How old is he?" Christy asked, sounding motherly.

"He's only 18," Paula said, flipping her hair back.

"Paula!"

"What?"

"You're only 14."

"I'll be 15 in seven weeks and two days," Paula said, snatching the picture.

"Well, still, Paula!"

"What?" She looked at Christy with her lips pressed together.

"I think there might be some other guy out there that you could go after."

"Like who?"

"Like, well . . . I don't know! But you and an 18-year-old doesn't sound real good."

"It doesn't, huh? What about Todd? Did I start questioning you when you wrote and said you were going out with a 16-year-old California surfer whose best friend died from a drug overdose?"

"It wasn't a drug overdose, Paula. Shawn crashed into the jetty while he was body surfing."

"Right. Body surfing at night, and so stoned he didn't know what he was doing. Tell me how great that sounds, Christy."

"Paula! That was Shawn. Todd isn't like that. He's a Christian. And I'm a Christian now, too." She spit the words out, angry and hurt, yet feeling foolish for arguing this way with her lifelong friend.

"What's that supposed to mean? 'I'm a Christian now, too,' " Paula mimicked.

Christy pulled back, fumbling for some kind of answer while her heart pounded accusations through her veins. *Some Christian you are! Yelling at your best friend. Real Christians don't yell at their best friends.*

"Paula," Christy began slowly, "I'm sorry. Let me try to start again. When I say I'm a Christian now, what I mean is that I gave my heart and my life to Jesus Christ.''

Christy and Paula had always been able to talk about any-thing, but now she felt frustrated and unsure of how to explain something she barely understood herself. "My whole life I've felt as though God was all around me, you know what I mean?''

Paula nodded slightly.

"My beach friends explained that that's not enough. I needed to surrender my life to the Lord—to open the door and let Him in. So I asked God to forgive me for all the wrong stuff I've done, and I invited Jesus to come into my life. Then I promised Him my whole heart. Forever.''

Paula squinted her big blue eyes. "So what does that mean? Are you going to become a nun or something?''

"No!" Christy playfully tossed a pillow at Paula. "I don't really know how to explain it. It's as if God isn't just all around me anymore; now He's inside me.''

"Well, good," Paula said, suddenly sounding sweet but dis-tant. "I'm happy for you, Chris, really. Sounds like everything in your life is going the way you want it to.''

"I guess it kind of is," Christy said. "I still have so much to learn. All my beach friends are really super close to the Lord, and they talk to Him like He's their best friend. I don't feel that close yet. But then," Christy said with a smile, "I only started this re-lationship with Him a couple of days ago.''

Paula's phone rang, and she grabbed it on the first ring. "Hello? Hi, Melissa. What? Oh, please. Not that song again!'' Paula handed the phone to Christy. "Here, listen." Christy could hear the beat of an unfamiliar song as it pounded through the receiver.

Paula pulled the phone back and sang along in a whining voice, making fun of the song. Then she said, "I'm sick of that old song, Melissa. Aren't you? What? No, she's still here. Okay.

I'll call you when she leaves. When? I don't know. Pretty soon. Okay. Bye."

The remarks stabbed Christy's heart. She realized Paula had made friends this summer, too. They had both changed. Things weren't the same between them anymore.

Paula eyed the Disneyland bag Christy had dropped on the floor when she came in. "So, are you going to show me all your souvenirs from Disneyland?" Paula asked.

"Oh, yeah. Here," Christy said. "This is for you."

"Really?" Paula jumped from the bed and scooped up the bag. "I can't believe that on your big date to Disneyland with Todd, you actually thought of me!"

"Of course I thought of you. I thought of you all summer, Paula. You're my best friend."

Paula looked directly at Christy before opening the bag and said softly, "I honestly thought you had totally forgotten about me."

"How can you say that?" Christy wanted to add, "Did you think at all about me, Paula? Or were you too busy with Melissa at the Dairy Queen?"

"I love it!" Paula squealed, pulling the Minnie Mouse sweatshirt from the bag and holding it up. "How adorable! This is just what I asked you to get. Thanks, Chris!" Paula quickly slipped it on over her clothes. The oversized sweatshirt completely covered her shorts.

"What do you think?" Paula asked, modeling in front of her full-length mirror. "I'm going to wear it tonight to the party. Melissa is going to love it! If I would have thought of it, I would have asked you to get a matching one for her."

A matching one for her! The thought jabbed Christy and kept jabbing her as she shuffled home in the mucky heat of the late July afternoon. The smell of cows permeated the air, and a swarm of annoying little gnats buzzed around her head. Christy kicked at the pebbles in the dirt and muttered, "You should have gotten a matching one for Melissa."

Great, Paula. Just great. Go to your stupid party. Let Melissa be your best friend instead of me. Doesn't bother me a bit. I'm moving to California.

Then it hit her. Like a cruel slap in the face, Christy realized why her parents had been so tense last night when they picked her up from the airport and told her they had sold the farm. They really were leaving everything. Their lives would never be the same. She would no longer live close to Paula, and they'd never again go to the same school. She was leaving for good. Everything was about to change.

Then the final blow, the stunning realization, hit her full on: *Even if we weren't moving to California, even if everything were the same and we were still living here, I still just lost my best friend.*

CHAPTER TWO

The Land of If Only

Miserable. It's the only word that described how Christy felt when they pulled into her Aunt Marti and Uncle Bob's driveway in Newport Beach, California. Here she was, in her wonderful, California dream locale, and she hated everything and everybody. The whole family seemed to feel the same way.

They had been traveling cross-country for seven horrible, miserable days. And now, stumbling into Bob and Marti's luxurious beachfront home, they continued to gripe and complain, as if being there were some kind of disease inflicted on them.

"Anyone hungry? Sleepy? Ready for a shower?" Uncle Bob, a handsome, easygoing man in his early fifties, offered his usual hospitality and received only grunts in return.

Christy's dad, a large man with bushy eyebrows and thick reddish brown hair, carried in the last of the luggage. Her eight-year-old brother, David, planted himself cross-legged in front of the TV. He was a smaller version of their dad and was, in Christy's opinion, annoying in every way.

Christy went to the open sliding glass door that looked out onto the wide, sandy beach and, beyond that, the Pacific Ocean. The sun had set, but the sky retained a streak of gold clouds, with enough light to see the silhouettes of a few surfers catching a final wave.

Down the beach to the left, Christy spotted a campfire starting up and the outline of a small group standing around the fire
ring, probably roasting hot dogs.

She drew in the damp, salty evening air, and for the first time
in days, something besides anger and frustration stirred inside
her. Little bits of memories ignited, like kindling in the campfire.

Her heart warmed, her spirits rose, and she felt drawn to the
small group down at the beach. It might be her friends from this
summer. They would be so surprised to see her! *Todd! Todd might
be there*, Christy thought. *Oh, I can't wait to see him again. Maybe he
brought his guitar, and I can hear him sing.*

"Dad?" Christy called out, gliding into the kitchen with re-
newed hope. "Mom? Could I go out on the beach for a little
while?"

Her parents slumped at the kitchen table, looking drained and
aggravated. Marti, a petite woman with short, dark hair and a
striking, polished appearance, stood in front of the open refrigerator. Bob was pushing the buttons on the microwave, warming
up some food for them. It was obvious by the expressions on their
faces that no invigorating sea breeze had stirred their souls the
way it had revived Christy's. Still, she had to ask.

"I just want to go down to the fire pits and see if my friends
are there. Could I? Please?"

"'Course not!" Dad snapped. "It's the middle of the night.
You didn't let Christy go out alone after dark when she stayed
with you, did you?"

"Well, actually," Aunt Marti began, "there were other young
people, and—"

Bob cut in. "You like drumsticks or thighs, Norm?"

"Whatever you've got left. Either one is fine."

"Christy," Bob continued, "did you notice the new wallpaper
in the den? We got it up just last week."

"Christy was here when we were trying to decide," Marti added, reaching for a bottle of flavored mineral water. "Do you two like orange and passion fruit?"

"Doesn't matter. Whatever you have." Mom's voice sounded beyond weary. Her short, brown hair lay flat against her head, and her round figure fit snugly in the kitchen chair.

Christy realized it was hopeless. If she asked again to go out on the beach, she would only cause a problem. Her uncle had conveniently helped her avoid what could have been a major confrontation. She better not press it.

Squelching all her hopes and anxious feelings deep inside, she sat with the adults, silently nibbling on a chicken drumstick. She told herself that tomorrow she could walk barefooted in the sand, and she would see all her friends; then she would feel alive again.

The next morning, Uncle Bob, wearing a Hawaiian print shirt and gray shorts, greeted her in the kitchen. "Good morning, Bright Eyes!"

"Morning!" Already dressed in her bathing suit and a big T-shirt, Christy slid into an oak chair at the table, where the sun streamed through the window like golden syrup.

"Ready for an omelette and raisin toast?" Bob asked.

"Sure!"

"It's absolutely terrific having all of you out here. Marti and I have wanted this for years," Bob said as he expertly flipped an omelette onto a plate.

"I don't know if my family feels the same way," Christy said quietly, pouring herself some orange juice from the pitcher on the table.

"Why do you say that?"

"Well, my mom has acted super strange ever since we left Wisconsin. And my dad, well, I don't know. The trip out here was horrible, and we all said some pretty mean things. But a couple of days ago, my dad said this whole move was a big mistake."

Bob set the steaming omelette in front of Christy and said, "Don't worry about it. He'll change his mind after the interview today at Hollandale Dairy. You'll see."

"I hope so." Christy smeared butter on her raisin toast and said in a low voice, "I kind of feel as though this is all my fault."

"Your fault? How could other people's moods be your fault?"

"I don't know. Because everything is turning out so awful, and I wanted them to like California as much as I do."

"Give them some time, Christy. Are you writing all these things down in your diary?"

"What diary?"

"I thought all teenage girls kept diaries," Bob said.

"I don't have one."

"I'll get you a diary today," Bob promised. "You should try to write in it whenever you can. It'll help you figure out yourself while you're going through all these changes."

Christy ate a few bites in silence. *Why is it that I can talk to my uncle so easily, but I can't talk to my parents? I wish I could talk to them about stuff the way I talk to Uncle Bob.*

"Thanks for the omelette. I don't think I can eat any more, though. We kind of didn't eat a lot on our trip out here, and I think my stomach shrunk or something."

"No problem."

"Uncle Bob, do you mind if I take some drinks and stuff down to the beach?"

"Of course not. Help yourself."

"I wanted to be the first one down there and surprise my old friends, if any of them are around," Christy said, clearing her dishes.

"I meant to ask you about Todd. Did he write or call much?"

"No," Christy said flatly. "That turkey! I wrote him three

times, but I had to send the letters to his mom's in Florida because I didn't have the address here.''

Christy pulled a beach towel off the shelf in the laundry room
and grabbed a drink and some grapes from the refrigerator. "Do
you think my parents will mind if I go out on the beach? They're
still asleep, and I don't want to wake them.''

"I'll handle your folks. Piece of cake.'' Bob winked at her, and
she smiled back.

"Thanks, Uncle Bob.''

"Listen, why don't you plan on checking back in at lunchtime.
The rest of the household should be up and at 'em by then.''

"Okay,'' Christy agreed and headed for the sliding glass door,
eager to slip out before anyone else woke up.

"Have a good time with your friends!'' Bob called after her.

Christy eased her bare feet into the golden sand and hurried
toward the ocean, drawn by the endless waves rolling in and out
with their crashing, foaming majesty. The sky seemed to blend
right into the horizon like a seamless blue robe gently draped over
the world and propped up by the wild ocean breezes.

I'm here. I've come back, she called out silently to the clear morning sky. Then prancing along the shoreline, she played tag with
the waves, daring them to erase her footprints.

*So, this is going to be my new home. Of course I'll adjust. I'll love
going to school with all the friends I made this summer.* The frustrations
and agony of being uprooted and moving out here began to wear
away, washed by the morning tide.

I'm here! Todd! I'm back.

Christy excitedly scanned the water for Todd's familiar orange
surfboard. Five surfers bobbed over the morning waves, but Todd
wasn't one of them. All she could do was wait. She spread out her
towel, dug her toes in the sand, and settled in.

Soon a girl's voice behind her called out, "Christy?''

She turned to see one of her summer friends, Leslie, tanned and smiling, her long, wavy hair flipping behind her in the wind.

Christy jumped up. "Hi!"

"Christy! I can't believe it's you!" Leslie said, giving her a hug. She propped her beach chair next to Christy's towel and said, "So what are you doing here? This is such a surprise."

Christy sat down and explained that her family had moved out here for good.

"I don't believe it! When did you get here?"

"Last night. Around 8:00."

"You're kidding!" Leslie's gray eyes grew wide. She leaned back in her low beach chair.

"No. Why?"

"Oh, you're not going to believe this, Christy! You could've come to our barbecue last night. We didn't know you were here."

"That's okay," Christy said.

"No, Christy, it's not okay. You're going to die when I tell you!"

"What?"

"The barbecue last night was a big going-away party for Todd. He left early this morning for his mom's in Florida!"

"No!" Christy wailed. Inside, all the dreams she had of seeing Todd again instantly shriveled up.

"If you would've shown up last night at the fire pit . . ." Leslie shook her head, and Christy forced herself to hold back the tears that begged to pour themselves out.

"I can't believe you were here the whole time! To think that you were only a few blocks away from where we were all sitting around the campfire . . ." Leslie must have noticed Christy's tears and suddenly tried to change the direction of their conversation. "You know, Todd really missed you after you left."

Christy blinked and swallowed and blinked some more.

Leslie seemed to be searching frantically for the right thing to say. "You know, Todd told me you were the best thing that had happened to him this summer."

"Did he really?" Christy asked in a whisper.

"Yes, he really did." Leslie smiled and spoke more calmly. "I don't know why it didn't work out for you two to see each other last night, but don't let it destroy you. You can drive yourself crazy living in the 'Land of If Only.' "

"The what?" Christy asked, blinking and sniffing quietly.

"I heard this lady talk once about how you could spend your whole life in the 'Land of If Only' by always looking back and saying, 'If only I'd done this,' or 'If only I hadn't done that.' It can really mess you up if you're always wishing things were different than they are. She said that when things happen that you don't understand, you have to believe God is still in control and nothing happens by mistake."

Christy looked out at the ocean and shook her head. "You make it sound so easy to trust God for everything, Leslie. I'm not sure it's going to be that easy for me."

"It'll get easier the more you do it."

Just then a voice behind them called out, "Hey! Leslie!"

They turned to see Tracy and Heather. Both girls looked the same as they had during the summer: petite Tracy with her heart-shaped face, and skinny Heather with her wispy, blond hair that danced around her face.

"It is Christy!" Tracy said to Heather. "What are you doing here?"

They all hugged and began to tell Christy that she should have come to Todd's going-away barbecue the night before.

"Save your breath," Leslie said. "We've already been through all that."

"Did you see Doug already?" Heather asked, then zipped

down to the water, waving for Doug to come in from surfing.

"I wondered if that was him," Christy said, watching the tall, broad-shouldered surfer emerge from the water. His short, sun-bleached hair stood straight up in the front. To Christy's surprise, when Doug recognized her, he ran to greet her, dropped his board, and gave her a big, saltwatery hug.

"Christy! Man, what a surprise! How are you? Wow, this is totally awesome!" Suddenly, his exuberance turned to a look of disappointment. "Oh, man! You should've been here last night when we had the—"

A chorus of female voices cut him off. "She knows!"

"Whoa! Excu-u-use me!"

"So, tell us what's happening, Christy. How come you're back?" Heather asked.

For the next few hours they all sat around, talking and laughing. The sun pounded their shoulders with its late summer fierceness, and the waves, like an uneven metronome, beat the shore in time with their conversation. It felt indescribably wonderful to be here. Another one of their friends, Brian, snuck up behind Heather and shook his wet hair all over her back.

"You gweek!" Heather shouted.

"Gweek?" Brian questioned.

Christy could see shy Heather beginning to blush. "Yeah, gweek!" she lashed back.

"Now there's a new word. Did you go to the library to look up that one?"

"As a matter of fact," Heather said slowly, obviously trying to think fast, "I went to the library and looked up 'gweek.' It said, 'prehistoric, total nerd-ball,' and then it had a picture of you, Brian!"

They all burst into laughter except Brian, who said, "Okay, Heather. You asked for it!" He pulled her up by the wrists and hollered for Doug to grab her ankles. In an instant, the two guys had hustled the screaming, kicking Heather down to the water and, on the count of three, tossed her in.

"Do they like each other?" Christy asked Tracy.

"Who? Brian and Heather? Who knows? They have a great time like this, but if they tried to go out, it would probably be a disaster. I don't think Brian will ever ask her out. Why ruin such a great friendship?"

"Kind of a strange way of looking at things," Christy said.

"I don't know. Sometimes I think dating is a strange way of looking at things. It's so much more fun being friends with a bunch of people and all going places together," Tracy answered matter-of-factly.

Leslie leaned over from her beach chair and said, "Tracy hasn't fallen in love yet. Wait until she meets a guy she's ga-ga over. She won't be so crazy about group dating then."

Heather scampered up from the beach, drenched but glowing. "I can't believe he did that!" she stammered.

Leslie, Tracy, and Christy exchanged glances that said, "Oh, sure!"

"Come on, you guys!" Heather said. "Let's go in the water! The guys are already out there."

The four of them clumped together and laughed all the way to the shoreline. When Christy first encountered the Newport Beach waves at the beginning of the summer, they had intimidated her—overwhelmed her. The day she met Todd, an angry wave had rolled Christy up into a little ball and literally pitched her at Todd's feet.

Today, she faced the waves with boldness. Her tall, slender frame ran toward them, slicing into their fury with the grace and agility of a young dolphin. Bobbing above the foam on the other side of the crest, she felt as if her face and hair shimmered in the sparkling field of water diamonds.

"I love this!" She flung the words into the air.

Tracy and Heather laughed as they bobbed beside her.

"You've been away too long," Tracy said.

"Come on," yelled Heather. "Let's catch this wave. Look at it!"

They kicked and thrashed through the water that swelled behind and before them until the mighty wave lifted them like a handful of arrows, shooting them toward the shore. Heather and Leslie rode it nearly all the way, but Christy and Tracy collided with each other, tumbling to shore like a pair of tennis shoes in the dryer. When they all caught their breath, they laughed hysterically at how the wave had pulled and twisted their hair into wild, wet, sandy styles.

"You should see your hair, Christy!" Heather squeaked like a toy mouse. "If you sprayed it purple right now, you'd have the perfect punker look!"

Christy laughed with them, patting down the stiff rooster's comb on top of her head. Then she turned around and went back for more tumbling and bodysurfing, while the guys raced them on their body boards.

Sometime later, breathless and with their bathing suits filled with sand, they retreated to their towels. Christy reluctantly asked the time.

"Probably close to 2:00," Tracy said.

"Yikes! I'd better go up to the house and check in. I'll be back later, if I can." Christy gathered up her things and said good-bye to her friends.

Oh, how she wished Todd were with them today! Would he read her letters when he got to Florida? Would he ever write her back? Most of all, she wondered if what Leslie said was true. Did Todd really think she was the best thing that had happened to him this summer?

CHAPTER THREE

Dear Diary

Christy's mom and Aunt Marti were stretched out in lounge chairs on the front patio, shaded by a big yellow-and-white umbrella. Both looked up when Christy came in from the beach.

"Good morning!" Christy greeted them brightly.

"Try 'Good afternoon,' " Marti said, spreading her full lips to reveal a contented smile. She looked young in her crisp white shorts and black knit top. Never before had Christy realized how much the two sisters, her mom and Aunt Marti, were worlds apart. Seeing them side by side in Marti's domain made her mother look like the frumpiest, plainest, dullest woman in the world.

Her mother's graying dark hair lay flat against her head, whereas Marti's dark, full hair framed her face perfectly. Christy's mom's face looked wrinkled and bland, without a spot of makeup. Marti's smooth skin was enhanced by bright lipstick and dramatic eye makeup.

Now that we're in California, maybe Mom will let Marti change her from a farmer's wife to a socialite, Christy thought.

Christy smoothed her towel over a patio chair and sat eye-level with her mom and aunt.

"Christy!" Mom yelped, getting a good look at her face.

"Look at you! You're burned to a crisp!"

Christy touched her cheeks. "It's not that bad."

"Dear, you should always use sunscreen on your face, remember?" Marti said sweetly.

"I did," Christy said.

"Do you need some more of the sunscreen I bought you?" Marti asked.

"Did it come off when you went in the water?" Mom said.

"Oh, this is great!" Christy teased. "Now I have two mothers telling me what to do all the time!"

"Every girl on this planet should be so fortunate," Marti returned with her self-confident grin. "Did you have a nice time with the other young people on the beach?"

"Yes." Christy settled back in her chair. "Some of my old friends were there, but not all of them." She didn't know if her aunt had said much about Todd to her mom, and she wasn't sure she wanted to bring up the subject. Her parents might really be upset if they knew that she had gone to Disneyland alone with Todd and that he had driven. With all the franticness of moving, Christy hadn't told her parents much about Todd.

"You should've met this one friend of Christy's," Marti said to her sister. "Absolutely a doll! The kind of teenager that makes you feel there's hope for our future."

That's sweet, Aunt Marti. I didn't know you felt that way about Todd.

"Her name was Alissa."

Oh . . .

Marti touched her sister's arm for added emphasis. "Gorgeous girl. Had a very refining effect on Christina, I'm sure."

All the aggravating feelings Christy ever had for her aunt returned like a monstrous wave, crashing her spirits with its force. *You are so clueless, Aunt Martha! Alissa has more problems than anyone*

I ever met! Todd and his friends were the ones who influenced me the most. Not Alissa!

"Did you see her today?" Mom asked.

"Who?"

"Alissa, this nice girl Marti liked."

"No, she's back in Boston at her grandmother's."

"You know," Marti said, springing from her chair, "I think Bob said a letter came for you from Boston. Let me see if it's in the den."

Marti scampered off, and for just an instant Christy smiled at her mom. *Maybe I don't want Marti to remake you. Maybe I need you to be the plain, old mom that you are.*

"The men went to San Marcos to check out the dairy," Mom said. "I hope everything turns out okay."

"Where's San Marcos?" Christy asked, taking a sip of her mom's iced tea.

"I think Bob said it was about an hour and a half drive south of here, toward San Diego."

An hour and a half! Christy nearly spit out the tea. "You mean the dairy is more than an hour's drive from here? I thought it was right around here."

"Christy!" Mom looked surprised. "You knew we weren't going to live here."

"I knew we weren't going to live *here*, with Bob and Marti, but I thought we were going to live in Newport Beach."

Her mother shook her head. "Sometimes, Christina, I think you live in a dream world. You only hear the things you want to hear. We could never afford to live here. If the job works out for your father, Bob has a friend in real estate who will rent us a house in Escondido."

Christy couldn't believe what her mother was telling her. "Where's Escondido?"

"Near San Marcos, of course. The house is in the older section of town, and the rent is what we can afford."

"Where will I go to school?" Christy had pictured herself starting school next week with at least one of her beach friends in some of her classes. Now the thought of beginning a brand-new school without knowing a single person absolutely horrified her.

"We'll figure all that out once we get to Escondido."

No! No! No! No! Why can't we live here? Why didn't anyone tell me the dairy was so far away?

Like a complicated machine grinding to a halt, Christy's thoughts froze. *Maybe Dad's job will fall through, and we'll have to go back to Wisconsin.* Then, without warning, her thoughts spun forward. *What am I thinking? I want to live here, not Wisconsin!* Mentally, she scrambled to find the "off" switch.

"I was right!" Marti announced, swishing a letter in the air. "Here it is, Christy. Listen, your mother and I were just about to run some errands. I've got to go to Corona del Mar first, then we can browse through a few shops on the way back. Why don't you hurry and get cleaned up? I need to get to the dry cleaners before 4:00."

"I don't know . . . " Christy fumbled with the words, knowing how her aunt didn't like others bucking her plans. "If it's okay with you, Mom, I'd kind of like to stay here instead."

"Why?" Marti demanded.

"Well, it was a long trip out here, and I'd like to unwind a bit." The words didn't even sound like hers. Christy had grabbed frantically for an explanation that would satisfy her "two moms" because she needed some time alone to think.

"Actually, that sounds sensible, Christy," Mom said, standing up. "I'm going to run a comb through my hair, Marti, then I'll be ready to go."

"Why don't you change, too? We have time."

Christy's mom looked down at her slightly crumpled navy blue cotton skirt and her white cotton blouse. "This is all right, isn't it?"

Christy couldn't believe it! Marti had played the same game with her this summer, but Christy never thought Marti would torture her own sister with the "you-don't-look-good-enough-to-be-seen-with-me" game.

"Suit yourself," Marti said briskly. "I'll grab my things and pull the car out."

"Have fun!" Christy called after them. She knew what their afternoon would be like with Marti at the control panel. She knew it would be an education for her mom. She also knew it probably wouldn't be fun.

Stretching out on the vacated lounge chair, Christy slit open the envelope with her thumbnail and pulled out a one-page letter from Alissa.

Dear Christy,

I received your letter today and was happy to hear from you. I'm still with Bret. He's a wonderful guy. Too good for me, really. My grandmother loves him and invites him over constantly. I'm almost afraid to break up with him because my grandmother would miss him too much! Just kidding. Part of your letter intrigued me. You said you'd "given your heart to Jesus" and that you felt that if I would do the same, my life would change.

What I don't understand is how you give your heart to someone who's dead. I believe Jesus was a good man, a good example—like Buddha and Mohammed. But why in the world would you make promises to a man who no longer exists? And how could that possibly change your life?

I'm not putting you down, Christy. If that's what you believe,
it's your own choice. But it certainly doesn't make any sense to me.
I can't understand why you would wish I would make the same choice.
Maybe I don't understand what you mean.

Please write when you find time.

Peace,
Alissa

Christy leaned forward in the lounge chair, nibbling on her
thumbnail, trying to think of how to answer Alissa. Her mind
went blank. She felt numb. There was too much going on inside
right now to think straight about anything.

"Just give me some time, Alissa," Christy whispered. "I'll figure this out." *If only we didn't have to live in Escondido. If only I could
stay here with all my Christian friends. If only—* Christy caught herself. *Oh, man! It's just like Leslie said. The Land of If Only. I think
she's right. I'd better stop it before I drive myself crazy.*

Christy pulled herself together and headed for the shower.
With each step up the stairs, she repeated Leslie's words, "God
is in control. God is in control." At the top of the stairs, she
stopped and smiled. "Lord, having You at the control panel is
going to be an education for me, isn't it? I just hope it's going to
be fun."

Christy wrote those very words in her diary that night before
going to bed. Bob had kept his promise and bought her a diary
that day. He gave her the brown leather-covered book after the
whole family had walked along the beach.

"Try to write in this diary every day, okay?" he prompted her.
"Write what you're feeling, what you're thinking, write down
what happens to you. Write your dreams, write your sorrows.
Don't neglect it. During these next few weeks, this little book
might become a real friend to you."

"Yeah," Christy had whispered, "it might be my only friend."

CHAPTER FOUR

The Slumberless Party

Escondido, Christy found out from Uncle Bob, means "hidden" or "hiding" in Spanish.

It fits, Christy thought when the family pulled up in front of the house that would become their new "Home Sweet Home." *This place is so hidden I doubt anybody will ever find me here.*

The house was small with a red tile roof and was tucked between six towering eucalyptus trees. The grass in front, withered and brown, had splotches of tall weeds that were bent and yellowed from the hot September winds. The screen door in front had a big rip in it, and a smashed clay pot lay strewn across the narrow front porch.

Mom surveyed the pathetic scene and looked as if she might cry.

"Hank said he'd meet us here at 11:00. We're a little early," Uncle Bob said, looking at his watch.

"You suppose this real estate tycoon would be willing to knock off a couple of bucks' rent if we agree to fix up this place?" Dad asked.

"Don't see why not. Let me talk to him," Bob said.

Someone in a bright red BMW honked and pulled into the driveway behind Bob's Mercedes. The car's door swung open, and a large man in a gray business suit hopped out. "Bobby-boy!" He greeted Christy's uncle and then quickly, vigorously, shook hands with all of them.

Christy noticed a girl with long, wavy blond hair sitting in the passenger seat of the BMW. She kept her back to the group of them standing on the dead lawn. A few minutes later Christy noticed that the girl had opened the sun roof so that the loud music from the radio poured out.

"Come on over and meet my little girl," the realtor said loudly. They all followed him to the car, where he tapped on the window. The thin, nice-looking girl rolled it down and then lowered the radio's volume.

"Brit," her dad said, "this is the Miller family. That's Davey over there, and this is Crissy."

"Christy," she corrected him softly. Nobody, but nobody called her "Crissy." Ever! Who was this clown, anyway? And what kind of a daughter did he have?

"Hi," the girl said with little expression on her face.

Christy returned the same level of enthusiasm with an equally flat, "Hi."

"You two get to be real good friends, now," the man said. "We'll go on inside. I've got the house keys right here, and I've got some rental papers for you folks to sign. This used to be a guest house, you know, for that large estate over there. Very historic area, this part of town."

They walked off and left Christy standing alone in the bright sun, feeling lost and humiliated.

The girl in the car turned the radio back up and tilted her seat back so her face was in the shade. She had a narrow face, high cheekbones, and deep gray eyes. Glancing up at Christy, she remained expressionless.

"Um . . ." Christy tried to find a starting point. "I don't think I got your name."

"It's Brittany," the girl said. "What was yours again?"

"Christy."

Silence hung between them as a hot wind made Christy's white T-shirt flap, drying some of the perspiration dripping down her back.

"Is it always hot here like this?" Christy asked.

"No. Only when we have the Santa Ana winds. Usually the first week of school is the hottest week of the whole year. It's really dumb. I don't know why they don't shut down and let everybody stay home till the end of the month when the weather is cooler."

"Where do you go to school?" Christy asked.

"Kelley High. You'll go there, too. What year are you?"

"A sophomore," Christy said.

"Me, too." Brittany looked a little more interested in Christy. "I wonder if we'll have any classes together."

"I'm not registered yet."

"Try to get Health with Ms. Archer. I was T.A. for her class last year. She's a modern teacher, if you know what I mean."

Christy didn't know what she meant. She didn't even know what "T.A." meant. She didn't want to ask. All she wanted was for Brittany to like her. To accept her. To be her friend.

That night Christy wrote about Brittany in her diary:

> I think I've found my first friend. Her name is Brittany. She reminds me of Alissa in some ways—intriguing and intimidating at the same time. She's the kind of girl I always think I want to be like, but when I'm around her, I feel as though I'm not on the same level.
>
> I think I'd like to be like her because Brittany seems so mature and experienced. Not clumsy, the way I am.

*Still, I don't know. I liked having Paula for my best friend because
we seemed to be the same in so many ways. At least we used to be. I
think I'd like to be more sophisticated, like Brittany.*

The next morning, Christy woke up early. Her room felt unbearably hot. She pushed her window open all the way, and the
desert winds fluttered the thin, white curtains. The overly spicy
fragrance of eucalyptus filled her room, smelling like the Aqua
Velva aftershave her dad wore on special occasions.

She slipped on a wrinkled pair of shorts and a sleeveless red
cotton shirt and then set to work, unpacking the last four moving
boxes in her room. By 8:30, everything had been unpacked and
arranged the way she liked it.

Her room didn't look too bad. It was much smaller than her
room on the farm, but the closet was bigger, which meant she had
no trouble getting all her clothes in.

On top of her antique dresser, she had arranged all her trea-
sures. The glass-blown Tinkerbell from Disneyland, the ceramic
music box with the cable car that moved up and down a little hill,
a framed picture of Paula and her from their eighth-grade grad-
uation, and in a Folgers coffee tin, her dozen, dried carnations
from Todd, which now smelled an awful lot like coffee and not at
all like spicy-sweet carnations.

Christy smoothed back the yellow patchwork quilt on her bed
and placed her Winnie the Pooh bear against the pillow.

"There you go, Pooh," she said cheerfully. "Your new home.
How do you like it? I know," Christy said, sitting on the bed and
taking Pooh into her arms. "I'm pretty scared, too. But we'll make
it. You'll see. God is in control. We just need some friends."

Two days later, Christy started her first day at Kelley High. To
her relief, she and Brittany had algebra together for third period.
They also had Ms. Archer's health class together for fourth

period. At lunch, Brittany introduced Christy to two other girls.

"This is Christy Miller," Brittany said. "She's new. Just moved here from Iowa or something."

"Wisconsin," Christy said softly.

"Wisconsin," Brittany repeated. "And this is Janelle and Katie Cougar."

"Oh, thank you very much!" Katie said in a sarcastic voice. "I suppose I am now labeled for life: 'Katie, the Kelley High Cougar.'"

Katie, a lively, athletic girl, wore her straight, thin, copper-colored hair in a short, blunt cut so that it swished like an oriental fan every time she moved her head. Her eyes looked like cougar eyes, bright green and flashing.

"She's our school mascot," Brittany explained.

Janelle started talking in a breathless, flighty sort of way. "Come on, Katie! Do one of your little cheers for us!"

"That's okay, Janelle. I'll save it for the rally on Friday," Katie said.

The three girls joked and talked while Christy silently looked on, eating her peanut butter and honey sandwich. She liked Katie and Janelle instantly.

Janelle wore her jet-black, curly hair loose around her face, which made her look as if she'd just flown in from somewhere exotic. Her bright personality matched her carefree appearance. Christy decided she would try with all her might to be accepted by this group of girls, especially Janelle.

To Christy's delight, she and Janelle were in the same Spanish class after lunch. Christy took a seat behind her. Everyone in the class seemed to know Janelle, and Christy felt excited about the idea of being friends with someone so popular.

It seemed that everything was turning out just right as the week went on. The girls included her in their little lunch group every day, and Brittany even complimented Christy on an outfit she wore on Thursday that her aunt had bought her last summer.

"It makes you look so thin," Brittany said.

Then, Friday at lunch, Christy knew her worries about making friends were over. Janelle announced that she was having some friends over to stay the night and she included Christy in the group of girls she invited. Inwardly, Christy congratulated herself and thought how easy it had been to get in with a popular group of girls. Janelle enthusiastically told everyone, "Bring some t.p. with you!"

"Some what?" Christy asked Brittany.

"T.p. You know, toilet paper!" Brittany answered.

"Oh." Christy looked to the other girls for an indication of what they were talking about.

Janelle held their attention with her lighthearted giggle. "We're going to get his house better than last time!" she declared, and all the girls around her went on about some guy named Rick Doyle.

Oh well, guess tonight I'll find out what all this is about.

That afternoon, Mom was hesitant about letting Christy go to the party until she found out that Brittany would be there. Mom insisted on talking to Janelle's mother on the phone to make sure the party would be supervised.

Then, that night, Mom actually walked Christy to the front door to check out the whole situation before completely agreeing that Christy could stay. It was so embarrassing.

The worst part was when Christy's mom said, loud enough for some of the other girls to hear, "Now, if you have any problems, Christy, you call me. Even if it's the middle of the night. Okay?"

Christy nodded and breathed a sigh of relief when Janelle's mom said, "They'll be fine," and shut the front door.

I can't stand being treated like a baby! I hope the other girls didn't hear all that, Christy thought. *When I'm a mother someday, I will never, ever treat my children that way!*

Christy's thoughts were interrupted by Janelle's contagious laugh. "How many did you bring, Christy?"

"How many what?"

"Rolls of t.p."

Christy was confused, but Brittany interrupted and said, "Look, you guys! I'm ready for Rick's house!" She pulled two jumbo packs of toilet paper from the center of her sleeping bag.

"That's great!" Janelle squealed. "How many did you bring, Christy?"

Christy meekly pulled her one roll of toilet paper from her overnight bag and said, "I don't mean to sound really dumb or anything, but what are we going to do with the toilet paper?"

"Go papering!" Janelle giggled. "Haven't you ever been papering before?"

"No."

"You only do it to people you like," Brittany explained. "Like really cute guys."

"Like Rick Doyle," Janelle added.

Brittany must have read the confused expression on Christy's face, because she continued her explanation. "See, in the middle of the night, we'll all go to Rick's house and really quietly string toilet paper in the trees and around his car and around his bedroom window."

"Why?" Christy asked.

Janelle laughed and echoed Christy's why. "Because . . . I don't know! We just do it for fun and try not to get caught."

"Sounds like fun." Christy tried to get her spirits up and bouncy the way everyone else's seemed to be.

"Okay, you guys," Katie called from the crowded living room. "Everybody's here. Let's get the games going."

They all sat on the floor, and Janelle gave each of them a small piece of paper. She told them to write down their most embarrassing moment without writing their names and then put their folded pieces of paper into the bowl.

Janelle kept giggling as Christy tried hard to think. Finally, she wrote about the time last summer when she was learning to body surf with Alissa, and a huge wave took her under and landed her on the shore, covered with seaweed, in front of Todd and a bunch of his surfer friends.

Once they had all put their papers into the bowl, Katie drew them out one by one and mercilessly read them aloud to the group. Everyone tried to guess to whom the incident happened.

Janelle laughed the longest and hardest of anyone, especially about her own. Hers was from junior high when she dressed in a hurry after P.E. one day and forgot to put on her skirt. She felt as though she were dressed because of her half-slip. Hurrying out of the girls' locker room, she ran past the entire guys' P.E. class, got all the way to her English class and in her seat before the guy next to her said, "Hey, did you forget something?" Then she had to run all the way back to the girls' gym to get her skirt.

Christy turned several shades of red when hers came up. "It has to be Christy's," Brittany said. "Look how embarrassed she is just listening to Katie read it."

"That must've been awful," Katie said, "ending up on the beach in front of all those guys!"

"It was!" Christy agreed. "But the good part was that's how I met Todd."

"Ooooh!" the girls all teased. "Tell us about Todd!"

"First let's finish this game," one of the girls urged.

The next one Katie read was her own. Everyone guessed it before she finished reading. Her most embarrassing moment was when she tried out for mascot the year before. Her shorts ripped in the back, right in front of the judges. She didn't know it and kept right on going, finishing the whole routine with her bright pink underwear flapping in the breeze.

"I need a new most embarrassing moment," Katie moaned. "You guys already know my life story!"

Of all the stories, Christy thought Brittany's was the most embarrassing. She wrote that at a pool party last summer at her house, she dove into the pool, and her bikini top came off. She treaded water in the corner of the deep end while Janelle tried to get it. But the strings got tangled in the pool filter, and Brittany's dad had to retrieve the top.

"It was the worst!" Janelle said.

"Were there any guys at the party?" someone asked.

"Yes!" Brittany said. "Only about eight of the cutest guys in the whole world!"

"Was Kurt there?" Katie asked.

"Please don't ever mention that name around me again!" Brittany said dramatically.

"Kurt is a jerk," Janelle added.

"Wait a minute," Katie said. "I thought you two were still together."

"No way! We broke up before school even started."

"Okay, okay! So I'm a bit behind on the latest romance scandals around here. I'll have to renew my subscription to the *Kelley High Tattler*."

The girls all laughed, and the game seemed to have officially ended. For the next hour or so, they munched on the snack food as half a dozen conversations whirled around Christy. She sat quietly sucking the sugar coating off the peanut M&M in her mouth.

Had these girls really accepted her? Was she part of their group now? She felt like it, even though the things they talked about were more intense than what she and Paula would talk about. A few of these girls dressed as though they were 20 instead of 15. Several of them had fashionable, mature-looking hairstyles and wore excessively wild makeup. Christy's parents had agreed to let Christy use some of the makeup Aunt Marti bought her last summer. Their only rule was, "If we can tell you have makeup on, you're wearing too much." So far, there had been no problems.

"Come here, you guys," Katie called from the kitchen. "Janelle's calling Rick!"

"Is your refrigerator running?" Janelle disguised her voice over the phone. "Then you'd better go catch it!"

She clicked the receiver down and broke into a burst of her wild laughter. "He's home all right! He asked if I was on drugs."

"Janelle, you're so crazy," Katie said. "I can't believe you did that! That has to be the oldest phone prank around."

"Oh come on, Katie. You just wish you were the one who called him instead of me."

Who is this Rick, and why are they so crazy about him? Christy thought.

Shortly after midnight, Janelle announced they were ready to go. Christy followed the others as they piled into the back of Janelle's parents' motor home.

"I can't believe your mom agreed to drive us," Christy whispered to Janelle.

"She loves this. My mom did much worse stuff when she was a teenager. She thinks this is great."

The motor home slowly drove past a big Spanish-style house with a red tile roof and a long front yard with bushes to the side and two birch trees by the street.

"That's it," Janelle whispered. "Park down the street, Mom."

Christy followed the rest of the girls as they quietly hopped out of the side door of the motor home. They ran like timid deer to Rick's front yard, with the rolls of toilet paper stashed under their shirts. She watched the other girls unwind their t.p., draping it over the bushes, throwing it into the big tree, and waiting for it to come down on the other side.

Slowly, cautiously, Christy unrolled her t.p. in a long line over the top of the bushes along the side of the yard. In the shadows, she spotted Janelle tiptoeing to the front of the house, where she bravely zigzagged the paper across the front door.

Another girl tied a precarious bow onto the mailbox. With hushed whispers, the girls completed their task. Then Katie and Janelle slipped around the side of the house to what Janelle insisted was Rick's bedroom window. They tried to weave the t.p. across his window. It wasn't working very well, and they hoarsely squabbled over what they were doing wrong.

All of a sudden the bedroom light flicked on. Katie screamed. Then Janelle screamed. Then they ran. Their terror set off a chain reaction among the group waiting in the front yard. Girls started running in every direction. In her panic, Christy ran behind some bushes and hid.

Then two things happened. First, the porch light snapped on, and a tall man in pajamas swung the door open, sliced through a spider web of toilet paper, and charged into the darkness with a baseball bat.

At the same time, to Christy's horror, she saw the motor home zooming past the house with all the shrieking girls inside.

They left me! No one told me to run instead of hide. What am I going to do? Christy thought hysterically.

"Rick!" the tall man bellowed from the front door. "Come see what your fan club left you."

A tall, broad-shouldered guy with thick, curly brown hair appeared in the doorway, wearing flannel shorts and a T-shirt.

"Not again!" he moaned.

"They're getting pretty brash, Rick. Your mother woke me up

and said she heard a burglar outside our bedroom window.''

"Can I clean it up in the morning, Dad?"

"Nope. Do it now," the man said.

Then they both disappeared into the house.

CHAPTER FIVE

Nobody Told Me to Run

What am I going to do! What am I going to do! Christy panted behind the bushes. *Should I run? Where would I go? I don't know where I am. Should I try to find a phone? Who would I call? I don't know Janelle's number. And right now I'd rather die than call my mother to come get me.*

Christy rose from her crouched position to see if the noise she heard could possibly be the motor home returning. It wasn't. It was the automatic garage door opener on Rick's garage door. He was coming out!

Christy ducked back in her hiding spot. *What am I going to do? What am I going to do?*

Rick began pulling the long strands of toilet paper from the tree and stuffing them into a garbage bag. He made his way all around the tree and then started for the bushes.

He's heading this way! What am I going to do? Christy's teeth chattered. She shivered uncontrollably, not from the cool night but from sheer terror. Rick now stood directly over her, briskly pulling the t.p. from the bushes.

She couldn't stand the suspense any longer. Without thinking, she gave in to the adrenaline pumping through her veins and popped up like a jack-in-the-box.

"Hi!" she squeaked.

"Ahhhhhh!" Rick dropped the bag of trash and stumbled backward. Quickly gaining his composure, he strained to see Christy's face, "Hey, who are you? What are you doing in there?"

Christy felt numbed by the bizarreness of the situation.

"Bye!" she squealed and took off running. She ran and ran and kept on running as fast as she could, with absolutely no idea where she was or where she was going.

The worst part was, Rick ran after her. "Wait! Stop! Come back!" he called.

But Christy kept running down the middle of the dark street. A car turned the corner and headed toward her. She moved closer to the sidewalk and kept running.

"Stop, will you!" Rick yelled. But his voice was drowned by the persistent honking of the car coming toward them. The lights began to flash, and Christy realized it was the motor home!

It slowed down, and Katie threw open the front passenger door. "Get in!"

In one awkward, flying leap, Christy threw herself into the front seat. As the motor home sped up, all the girls in the back pressed their faces against the windows, yelling and whistling at Rick.

Katie and Janelle shrieked with laughter in the front seat. "What in the world happened, Christy? Why was he chasing you?"

"Are you all right?" Janelle's mom asked.

Christy panted and rolled down the window for some air. The sweat dripped from her forehead and down the back of her neck. She had never felt so out of control. All she could do was laugh. A frantic, relieved, deep-chested laugh.

"Yes," she panted, "I'm all right."

The girls in the back all pushed into the opening to the cab and fired questions at her nonstop. "What happened?" "Why was Rick chasing you?" "What did you do?"

"I can't believe this!" Janelle squawked. "What happened, Christy? We didn't even know you were missing until we almost got all the way home. Everybody was talking and laughing, and then Katie said, 'Where's Christy?' and everybody freaked! Then, before we even got back to Rick's block . . .'"

Katie finished the sentence. ". . . there you were running down the middle of the street at 1:00 in the morning with Rick Doyle chasing you!"

Christy took another gulp of air and began to explain. "I didn't know you were supposed to run! When the light went on, I hid in the bushes. Then you guys left, and I couldn't move because Rick and his dad were standing right there."

"You're kidding! Then what happened?"

"I was going to try to sneak away, but Rick started cleaning up the toilet paper. When he came over to the bushes where I was hiding, I panicked."

"What did you do?"

"I-I . . ." Christy paused. "I can't believe I did this! It was so stupid!"

"What?" they all yelled.

"I stood up and said, 'Hi!' "

The whole group broke into uncontrollable laughter.

"I really scared him, too," Christy went on. "And then I got so scared, I started to run. He ran after me, and that's when you guys showed up."

"Did he know who you were?"

"No, it was too dark. Besides, he's never seen me before. When he was running after me, he kept yelling, 'Stop! Who are you?' "

"Does this sound like Cinderella, or what?" Katie teased.

They all fell into another round of riotous laughter.

"I can see him at school on Monday," Katie joked. "Rick will be trying the cardboard toilet-paper tube on the foot of every maiden in the kingdom!"

Christy felt herself blushing as they teased. She wasn't used to being the center of attention, but she loved it. They treated her as though she were some kind of heroine. Her escapade served as the highlight for the rest of the night. Katie said it was a tale that would probably be passed on for generations.

By 3:00 in the morning, all conversation had subsided on the living room floor. Katie and Janelle were stealing one of the girls' underwear from her overnight bag and giggling at their plans to freeze the bra.

In the darkness, Christy crept to the bathroom and opened the unlocked door. Only a night-light was on, but in the dim light, to her surprise, she saw Brittany kneeling over the toilet, throwing up.

"Brittany?" Christy whispered. "Are you okay?"

"Oh, yeah. I'm okay." Brittany rose to her feet and flushed the toilet, but the vile smell lingered in the air.

"Do you want me to see if Janelle has something for upset stomachs?" Christy asked, holding her breath. It always made her feel like throwing up whenever she heard someone else doing it or when she smelled it.

"No! No!" Brittany whispered urgently. "I'm fine."

"I'll go use the other bathroom," Christy offered and slipped down the hallway to the kitchen, where Janelle and Katie stood by the freezer. "I think Brittany might need some 7-Up or something. She was throwing up in the bathroom."

"See! I told you," Katie whispered to Janelle. "She's anorexic."

"Anorexics starve themselves. I see her eating all the time.

Didn't you see her eating all those brownies tonight?"

"Then she's the other thing," Katie accused. "Bohemia, or whatever—when they eat everything and then throw it all up."

"It's bulimia, Katie, and you can't prove that."

"I just think it's strange that she lost, like, 20 pounds this summer."

"She had a boyfriend," Janelle countered. "Kurt told her when they started going out that he liked skinny girls, so she shed a few pounds. What's strange about that? Now that they broke up, she'll probably gain it all back."

Christy felt completely left out of their conversation. When Katie and Janelle talked, their sentences almost overlapped each other because they were both so quick to answer the other.

"Well, I thought I should tell you in case she needs something later," Christy said.

"Okay, thanks," Janelle said.

Christy quickly used the other bathroom and returned to her sleeping bag. Brittany had moved her bag next to Christy's and lay stretched out, still awake. "So, tell me about your boyfriend, Todd."

Christy slipped her legs into her sleeping bag and asked softly, "Are you okay?"

"Of course. I'm fine. Are you and Todd still going together?"

"We never were really going together or anything," Christy explained. "We just spent a lot of time together this summer and got to know each other pretty well."

"Were you guys, you know, really close?" Brittany asked.

"Yes," Christy said with a sigh. "I really miss him."

"How involved were you?"

"Involved? What do you mean?"

"You know, like kissing and stuff."

"Well, he kissed me good-bye the day I left and gave me a

bouquet of carnations," Christy said proudly.

"That's it? One kiss? I thought you said you were really close." Brittany fluffed up her pillow and rolled onto her stomach.

"We were close. At least I felt close to him—sometimes." Christy thought back on their roller-coaster relationship. "I guess I felt so close to Todd because he's the one who really helped me become a Christian."

"You're a Christian?" Katie asked, overhearing them and pulling her sleeping bag over to join them.

"Yes," Christy said. "Are you?"

"Yes! So is Janelle." Katie called out softly across the room. "Hey, Janelle. You still awake?"

"Yeah." Janelle sat up in her sleeping bag across the living room floor. "What is it?"

"Christy just said she's a Christian! Isn't that great?"

Janelle flopped her head back down onto her pillow. "That's great," she mumbled.

Christy felt a little embarrassed that Katie had just announced to the whole room that she was a Christian.

"This summer I went to Hume Lake with Janelle and her church youth group," Katie said. "Hume is a fantastic camp. You'll have to go with us next summer. I loved it! On Wednesday night the speaker talked about how God loves us and wants us to be part of His family. I told my counselor that my life was too messed up, and I could never be good enough to be a Christian. She told me how it wasn't based on anything I could do; it was a matter of whether or not I wanted to accept God's free gift."

Christy enjoyed watching Katie's animation as she talked. It was as if her mouth wouldn't be able to move unless her hands were somehow in motion.

"That night I prayed and asked the Lord to come into my

heart and make me into a brand-new person. And He did! I feel as though I've started my life all over again. I can't believe how great it is being a Christian!"

"It's pretty great," Christy agreed. "But I don't know if my life has really changed all that much."

"Oh, mine has. My life was a mess. It still is—I mean my family is all messed up. But I don't feel all that agony inside anymore. I feel as though I'm part of God's family. He really, truly is like a father to me. For me, it was as if my heart melted when I asked Christ to come inside and pick up the pieces. I don't think I'd want my life to continue if God wasn't in it."

"Wow," Christy said softly. "I wish I felt that close to God. I know He's in my life, and I know He's interested and everything, but I don't really feel as if He's that involved. Do you know what I mean?"

"I'm not sure." Katie thought for a minute and then said, "You know, a couple of Sundays ago, the pastor at church said that if you want to grow as a Christian, you have to let the Lord into every area of your life. Otherwise, it's like inviting someone into your house and making him stand in the corner the whole time. If you never invite him to sit down or eat with you or do any of the things you'd do with a real friend, then you'll never get to know him."

Hmm. I wonder if Jesus is just standing inside my life, or if He's really free to move into every area? Everything is going pretty well right now. I guess He must be in there doing something to make everything work out so well.

"Do you want to go to church with us sometime?" Katie asked. "I get a ride with Janelle every week. I'm sure her family could pick you up, too."

"That'd be great!" Christy exclaimed. She noticed that Brittany was being awfully quiet, and she wondered if Brittany felt left out. Christy remembered how left out she felt last summer when her beach friends had talked about "the Lord" and she didn't know what they meant.

"Brittany?" Christy asked. "Do you want to go to church with us, too?"

She didn't answer. She was already asleep. Or at least pretending to be.

"Janelle invited her to go to Hume Lake last summer, but she didn't want to go because Kurt wasn't going. Maybe she'll come now that she's not with him anymore."

As their conversation wound down, Christy yawned and stretched out in her sleeping bag. Within minutes she was asleep.

The next morning around 9:30, Janelle's mom put out orange juice and donuts for the girls, but none of them was very hungry. They bumped around getting their sleeping bags rolled up and crabbed at each other about getting into the bathroom.

All Christy wanted to do when she got home was sleep. But instead, she was handed a rake. All day the family worked in the yard. They didn't finish, so they spent Sunday doing the same.

Monday at school the girls were still talking about the slumber party and greeting Christy as if she were the life of the party. Brittany even invited Christy to come to her house after school. It was encouraging to be liked and included.

Christy called her mom from school at lunch to ask if she could go home with Brittany. To her surprise, her mother said, "I suppose so. See if Brittany's mom can bring you home."

Brittany lived in a huge, ultramodern house with a swimming pool in the back, overlooking a lake.

"This is sure pretty," Christy said as she lay back in the padded lounge chair. "What lake is that down there?"

"Lake Hodges. It's not very exciting. You can't go water-skiing or anything. Just fishing." Brittany pulled her hair back in a scrunchie and took a sip of her diet soda. "Sure is hot today."

"Is your mom at work?" Christy asked.

"Who knows," Brittany answered flatly.

"What does that mean?"

"My mom moved out last spring. Last my dad and I heard, she was living in Paris."

"In Paris? Why?"

"She just flipped out. Went to go find herself or something, I don't know. She and my dad haven't gotten along for years. But I keep thinking she'll show up someday." Brittany sat up. "Do you want to hear something totally off the wall?" She went on before Christy could answer. "I have this dream that I'll come home from school one day, and Mom will be in the kitchen, Dad will be in the den reading the paper, and my brother will be back from college. We'll all sit down together to eat dinner, and everybody will be happy. Is that *Leave It to Beaver*, or what?"

Christy offered Brittany an encouraging smile. Everything within her ached for her new friend. Over the weekend Christy had argued continually with her brother. Their dad had yelled at both of them the whole time they were doing yard work (not that they didn't deserve it), and their mom had floated around in her lethargic mood. Christy thought her family was a mess, but compared with Brittany's, she had it made.

Christy ended up calling her mom and asking her to pick her up, which didn't please her mother a whole lot. When Mom found out Brittany was alone every day after school, she insisted that Brittany come over to their house.

It seemed to work out well. The girls got together at Christy's every afternoon that week, and Christy benefited tremendously from Brittany's help on her algebra. Christy hated math; but when Brittany explained it, it made sense.

On Thursday afternoon, Mom and David went to pick up

Dad while Christy and Brittany did homework at the kitchen table. Brittany got up to get a drink and bumped a butterfly magnet off the refrigerator. She picked it up and then told Christy, "My mom had a magnet like this on our refrigerator. She had all kinds of magnets. One of them was a little sign that said, 'One moment on the lips, forever wear it on the hips!'"

Christy laughed.

"One day," Brittany went on, warming up to the subject, "my dad gave my mom a magnet in the shape of a lamb that said, 'Ewe's not fat. Ewe's fluffy'; you know, 'e-w-e,' ewe."

"How cute!" Christy said.

"I thought so, too, but my mom got really mad at him and smashed the poor little lamb into a thousand pieces."

"Was your mom . . ." Christy hesitated. ". . . 'fluffy'?"

"No, not at all. She was super thin. She was always dieting, and she was always thin." Brittany paused a moment and then added, "She had a little help."

"What do you mean?"

Brittany lowered her voice. "She took some diet pills that the doctor prescribed for her."

"Oh," Christy said, unimpressed.

"She left a bottle when she moved out."

Christy didn't understand why Brittany was looking at her so intently, or why she was acting as though the diet pills were a big secret. She gave Brittany a look that said, "So?"

"Can you keep a secret?" Brittany asked.

"Yes."

"Don't tell anyone, but I took the bottle to the pharmacy, and they refilled it without even asking who I was or for a signature or anything."

Christy gave her another "So?" look.

"I've been taking the pills for a couple of months, and I've lost more than 20 pounds."

"I don't think you need to lose any more," Christy said.

"I'm not," Brittany said defensively. "I'm just telling you in case, well, if you might want to lose a few pounds. I could give you some of the pills. They're totally safe."

Christy sat still, her mind soaking up what Brittany was saying. For a long time Christy had been intrigued by those TV and magazine ads about losing weight. She thought she could stand to lose some weight, just around her stomach and her thighs. She never seriously considered taking anything to help her accomplish her goal; but the thought now made her heart race.

"I don't know," she stammered.

"If you don't like feeling hyper, there's something else you could take. That's what the diet pills do. They make you feel as if you have all this energy, and you only need about an hour's sleep every night. But when you crash, you really go out. Lately I've been taking laxatives. They work great. Make me feel healthy because they help clean out my system, especially when I've eaten a lot of junk food."

"You take laxatives?" Christy asked.

"Yes." Brittany tilted her chin down, turning her head and looking up at Christy like an innocent child.

"That sounds gross!"

"The kind I take are mild. You just swallow them like an aspirin. Here, I'll show you." Brittany opened her purse and lifted out a small box of laxatives along with a prescription bottle of diet pills.

"Why don't I give you some of these laxatives, and if you feel like losing a few pounds, you can take them. Or if you want to try the diet pills, I'll give you what's left in this bottle." She handed the prescription bottle and box of laxatives to Christy.

"There are only a few left in here, but I've got another whole bottle full if you want some more."

"I don't know," Christy said, scrunching up her nose. "I don't think I should."

Brittany gave her a motherly look. "They won't hurt you, Christy. It's not like taking drugs or anything. The best part is, since I've lost a few pounds, I've gotten more attention from guys than ever before in my life. Which reminds me of something. Did you see Janelle today after lunch?"

"No. Why?"

"She told me in English class that Rick Doyle found out she had the sleepover last Friday night. He came up to her in the hall and asked about you!"

"You're kidding!" Christy felt excited and nervous just hearing his name. "What did he say?"

"He said he wanted to find out who the girl was that ran away from him."

"What did Janelle say?"

"She had some fun teasing him. She didn't tell him your name. She said he'd have to find out on his own, and then she said, 'What's the matter, Rick? Are you so used to girls flocking in your direction that you can't handle it when one runs away from you?' "

"Oh, no!" Christy groaned, tilting her head down and staring at her algebra book. "I feel so stupid. I don't ever, ever, in my whole life want to meet him face-to-face."

"Oh, come on! You've got a wide-open invitation to catch the most desirable guy in school. And, Christy, if I can be honest with you, if you were to lose about five, maybe 10 pounds, the guy wouldn't be able to take his eyes off you!"

"Brittany!" Christy said in a long, drawn-out wail. "He's not interested in me, okay?"

Brittany ignored her and went back to work on her algebra, humming to herself.

Christy's mind raced. *Could Rick actually be interested in me? What if I were a few pounds thinner? Or what if I started wearing more makeup like Brittany and her friends?*

Somewhere deep inside of Christy the seeds were planted, and somehow she knew it was going to be very hard to ever be happy with herself the way she was.

If only I could lose some weight. Hmm . . . What would it be like to have a guy like Rick pay attention to me?

CHAPTER SIX

Just Say No

Christy ate dinner slowly, chewing every bite 20 times. She had read in a magazine at Brittany's house that counting her bites would help her eat less and lose weight.

David rattled on and on about his day at school and how some kid in his class got in trouble for cheating. Dad looked more tired than usual, but he wasn't grumpy, which was good. Mom looked as if she had something on her mind. After David excused himself from the table and planted himself in front of the TV, Mom asked Dad if he would like a cup of coffee.

Aha! Christy thought. *I knew you wanted to talk to Dad about something.*

Mom always used a cup of coffee as her buffer between herself and her husband when she had something to ask. Christy was still slowly chewing her 20 bites. Her mom didn't seem to mind if she stayed at the table. Maybe it would even give her mom more buffer.

"Norm, I've been thinking."

"Um-hmm," Dad answered, sipping his coffee.

"I think it would help out all around if I found a part-time job. Just while the kids are in school, of course. I could do some kind of secretarial work or maybe work at a fast-food restaurant."

"No wife of mine is going to wear a Burger King hat."

"Well, all right. I don't care what I do, but I need to find something. Yesterday, I called our landlord to ask if we could put in a fall garden, now that the yard is all cleaned up, and he said no."

"Why?"

"I don't know. I think he was having a bad day. The phone rang at his office about 15 times, and he was the one who finally picked it up."

"There's your answer," Dad said.

Mom looked at Christy, Christy looked at her dad. *Nineteen, 20,* she counted, then swallowed and looked back at her mom.

"What?" Mom asked. "What answer?"

Dad slowly took a swig of coffee. "The man obviously needs office help if he can't get someone to answer the phone for him. Go see him tomorrow. Tell him you'll answer his phones. What's his name? Hank?"

"I have his card," Mom said, jumping up and rummaging through a basket by the phone. "Here it is. Hank Taylor. Taylor-Made Properties. I wonder if he does need office help? Part-time, of course. Norm, what do you think?"

"Like I said, there's your answer."

Her dad's bluntness made Christy smile. *I hope Mr. Taylor hires her. That would be perfect! Then Brittany and I would get to do things together all the time.*

Not until she was in bed and almost asleep did she remember the laxatives and diet pills Brittany had given her. Brittany told her to take one or two before going to bed.

They were in her backpack, which she'd left in the living room. Of course, her parents were sitting on the couch, watching TV. They wouldn't go to bed until 10:00.

She tossed and turned. Brittany's voice echoed in her head: "Christy, if I can be honest with you, if you were to lose about five, maybe 10 pounds, the guy would not be able to take his eyes off you."

Maybe if I take only one, Christy reasoned. *What harm can one do?*

Then she remembered last summer when she said no to marijuana. This was different, but still, she never regretted saying no then. She knew she would have regretted it later if she'd tried even one puff. No, she didn't need to try diet pills or laxatives. Tomorrow she would throw them away.

She picked up Pooh bear and whispered in his ear, "And if Rick Doyle is truly interested in me, he can be interested in me, five extra pounds and all!" Christy hoped she could always convince herself of the same thing so easily.

The next morning, right before first period, Brittany met Christy at her locker, her eyes full of anticipation. "Well, how are you doing?" she asked with hidden meaning.

"Fine," Christy said brightly.

"How many did you take?" Brittany asked.

"Oh!" Christy caught on. "Those! I didn't take any. I didn't want to. You can have them back. Here." Christy reached in her purse for the prescription bottle. Brittany stepped in front of her and grabbed Christy's wrist.

"Not here!" she said through her teeth, looking over her shoulder at the crowd of students in the hallway. "Give them to me later, okay?"

Christy didn't talk to Brittany again until after school, but Brittany was too busy sharing the latest news flash on the school's hottest couples to ask for her diet pills back. "Did you hear that Janelle likes Greg now? He's a senior! Can you believe it? And you'll never guess who was waiting for me at my locker after school. Give up? It was Kurt. He said he'd been thinking about me. He put his arm around my waist and said, 'I see you've lost your baby fat.' And I told him, 'Oh, yeah? Well, you wouldn't know, would you?' And then he said he wanted to take me out this Friday, and I said, 'Only a fool would go out with you, Kurt, and I'm no fool.' "

"That was kind of cruel, don't you think?" Christy asked.

"After the way he messed up my life? Are you kidding? I would never go out with him again. I can't stand him! Once it's over, it's over, as far as I'm concerned."

"Can't you still try to be friends with him?"

"Why? He used me, Christy. That's how most guys are. They use you, and then they drop you. You can't squeeze a friendship out of that kind of treatment."

"Not all guys are like that," Christy said sharply.

"Oh yeah? What about Todd? Did he ever write you, like he promised?"

"Well, no. Not yet." Christy felt a familiar throb pounding in her throat. It came every time she thought about Todd. Maybe Brittany was right. Maybe he never would write to her.

"Guys are famous for making promises they never keep, Christy. You need to get Todd out of your mind. Forget about him and start concentrating on Rick. I heard today that Rick is still trying to find out who you are."

"Oh, really? Did he mention the way I 'ran into' him this morning in the hall?"

"No!" Brittany's voice perked up. "Tell me what happened."

Christy proceeded to tell her about the incident in the hall—how she ran right into Rick on her way to her locker. He acted as though he recognized her, but he didn't say anything, and she kept going without looking back.

"This is too good to be true!" Brittany said triumphantly. "You've got the guy hooked! Just think, by the time you two actually meet, you're going to be so thin you'll be totally irresistible to him.''

"Forget it, Brittany. It's never going to happen. Oh, and I just remembered something. My mom is thinking about getting a part-time job. Do you know if your dad needs anyone at his real estate office?"

"I don't know, but I'll ask him. He probably does."

That night after dinner Brittany's dad called and asked Mom to come in for an interview as a receptionist the next day. Mom acted strangely after she hung up the phone. She hadn't been able to get ahold of Mr. Taylor that day, and she seemed pleased yet somehow irritated that Christy had managed to set up the interview through Brittany.

About 20 minutes later, the phone rang again. This time it was Uncle Bob and Aunt Marti. Mom chatted excitedly about her upcoming interview, sounding confident and eager.

"Christy," her mom called out cheerfully, "come to the phone. Your uncle would like to speak to you."

"Hi, Bright Eyes. How's everything going for you?"

"Fine. How are you?"

"Good. We're doing real well. Listen, I've got a letter here that came for you."

"Really?" Christy felt her heart begin to race. "Who's it from?"

"I don't know; there's no return address."

Christy felt a burst of hope that the letter was from Todd. Then she remembered the last letter that had come for her at Uncle Bob's. "It's probably from Alissa," Christy said, feeling horribly guilty because she hadn't written Alissa back yet. She didn't have an answer to Alissa's questions about why Jesus was different than Mohammed or Buddha. She hadn't thought much about it, since she was so involved with her new friends.

"Could be," Bob said slowly. "I'll round up the carrier pigeon and shoot it off to you tomorrow. Hang on. Your aunt wants to talk to you."

"Christina dear, I just had a thought. Bob and I are going out to Palm Springs next weekend. Perhaps you and David would like to join us."

"Really?" Christy tried to think fast. She would love the chance to go to Palm Springs, but *not* with David! She lowered her voice and turned toward the wall so the others couldn't hear what she was saying.

"It's nice of you to ask, but it might not be much fun if you have to look out for both of us."

"Of course. How silly of me! You'd probably rather come with your friends. How much fun can you have with a little brother tagging along? Let's do this: You and some of your girlfriends come on this excursion, and then we'll take David and some of his friends on another outing, another time. Now let me talk to your mother and fill her in on the details. You'll have to miss school on Friday because Bob's golf tournament begins that morning. We'll pick you and your friends up on Thursday right after school. Does that sound good to you, dear?"

"It sounds great, Aunt Marti. I hope my parents will let me go."

"Of course they'll let you go. Here, put your mother on the line."

"Okay, here she is."

Christy went back to the sink and began rinsing off the dinner dishes.

"Really, Marti," she heard her mom say, "I don't think you have to do this." She was quiet for a moment; then she handed the phone to Dad.

He listened to Aunt Marti and threw in a "Well, really," then a "You folks don't need to."

But when he said, "All right, then," Christy knew she was going to Palm Springs. She felt like jumping up and down. *They're going to say yes! My parents are going to let me go.*

Suppressing her excitement, Christy wiped her hands off and tossed the dish towel on the counter. She turned to face her parents. They both looked the way they had months earlier when they said she could spend the summer with her aunt and uncle. That night they had made her promise that she wouldn't do anything that summer in California that she would regret telling them later.

Tonight their approach was a little different. "You can go," her dad said, "as long as you have all your homework done."

"No problem," Christy said lightheartedly. She felt as though they really trusted her, and it felt great.

"Now, Christy," her mom said, "this is awfully nice of them. I hope you realize that."

"I do," Christy said. "Thanks for letting me go."

"Marti said you could bring several friends. Why don't you invite Brittany?" her mom suggested.

"Okay. I thought I'd invite Janelle and Katie, too." Christy's imagination spun wildly as she pictured herself having an all-weekend slumber party with her new friends.

"Don't be disappointed if Janelle and Katie aren't able to go with you," her mom said.

"Why wouldn't they?"

Mom picked up the dish towel, folded it neatly, and placed it back on the counter. "Well, from what you've said about them, they seem to be very popular girls."

"They are."

"What I'm trying to say is that you don't have to try so hard to become friends with these popular girls. Sometimes the best friends can be the quiet, less-popular ones. Do you understand what I'm saying?"

"I think so," Christy said.

"Give it some thought," her mom said.

Her mother's words rumbled around in Christy's mind. *Is Mom saying that I'm not popular or that I shouldn't try to be popular? These girls really like me. They want me to be part of their group. Of course they'll want to go to Palm Springs with me. Why can't my mom see how important this is?*

CHAPTER SEVEN

From Pity Party to Pizza Party

The next day at lunch, Christy waited for Katie and Janelle in the spot where they all usually ate together. But neither of them showed up. She spotted Brittany across the grass, surrounded by four guys and too absorbed in them to notice Christy standing off by herself.

I can't believe this. Was Mom right? Are Janelle and Katie snubbing me? Christy sat down alone and yanked a pear out of her lunch sack. The fruit had so many bruises on it she couldn't find a spot to bite into without hitting mush.

Around her, clumps of people gathered. They were all talking and laughing, wrapped up in their private worlds. Christy felt like an alien. No, worse than that. She felt invisible. Like somebody could walk right through her and wouldn't even disrupt her molecules.

Why did Janelle and Katie leave me like this? What's wrong with me? I thought they liked me. I hate eating all by myself.

What made everything worse was that Christy could picture Paula, right now, eating lunch at their old high school. Paula would be sitting on the edge of the table, never on the bench, drinking her daily can of kiwi-strawberry juice and laughing. Except now it was Melissa, not Christy, who shared Paula's secrets and laughed at her antics.

Christy let herself drift off into the Land of If Only and for the rest of the lunchtime felt sorry for herself.

The shrill bell came as a welcome, nudging Christy to gather her things and wander off to Spanish class. She expected Janelle to come flying in and take the seat in front of her, but Janelle never showed up. She found out later from Brittany that both Katie and Janelle had gotten special permission to paint signs all afternoon for that night's football game.

They could've asked me to help, Christy thought. *I know how to paint.*

When Christy got home from school, she hid out in her bedroom. She threw herself on her bed and mentally listed all the reasons nobody seemed to like her.

She decided to try something. Standing up straight, she peered into the oval mirror above her dresser and projected her best "I'm-too-good-for-the-rest-of-you" look. No good. Her eyes had too much natural sparkle.

Next she tried a bright "Everybody-look-at-me-I'm-a-fun-person" look, but that didn't work either. When she smiled real big, all she saw were her large teeth. She didn't look full of carefree abandon, the way Janelle did when she smiled.

As she studied her next look, the "I'm-so-lonely-won't-somebody-please-feel-sorry-for-me-and-be-my-friend" one, David barged into her room without knocking.

"What do you want?" she hollered, spinning around. "Get out of my room!"

"Okay, okay," David said, stepping back two giant steps. He was officially "out" of her room.

"Would you close my door, please?" She preferred to have her pity parties in private.

"Okay. I guess you don't want to talk to the person on the phone. I'll go hang up for you."

"David!" Christy leaped across her room and elbowed her brother out of the way, managing to make it to the phone before he did. "Hello?" she answered breathlessly.

"Queen Christy doesn't want to talk to you!" David yelled toward the phone.

"David!" Christy covered the mouthpiece. "Get out of here!" She put the phone back to her mouth. "Hello?" she said sweetly.

"Hi, Christy!" Janelle said in her bouncy manner. "Are you going to the game tonight? I didn't see you today, so I didn't get to ask you. Katie needed help with some of her mascot duties, so I didn't go to Spanish. Did I miss anything?"

"Not really. We're suppose to work on the next dialogue for Monday." Christy felt a rush of joy. Her friends hadn't forgotten about her after all.

"Oh, yuck. I still haven't memorized the dialogue from last week," Janelle groaned. "Spanish is not my favorite subject, let me tell you. So, are you going to the game tonight?"

"I don't think so. I'm supposed to baby-sit my little brother."

"Well, try to get out of it. We could give you a ride."

"I'll have to ask. Could I call you back if it works out?"

"Sure. Wait a sec. . . . Oh, Katie just said that you wanted to go to church with us sometime. Do you want to go this Sunday?"

"Yes, I do, if that's not a problem."

"Of course not. We'll pick you up around 8:45."

"I really appreciate it," Christy said, feeling as though the whole world had changed from clouds to sunshine. Janelle actually included her in her evening plans for the football game! This would be an ideal time to invite her to Palm Springs.

"Janelle," Christy asked with a smile in her voice. "I was wondering if you'd like to go to Palm Springs next weekend."

"Are you kidding? Of course I would! Who's going?" Janelle answered without a moment's hesitation.

"My aunt and uncle are. They said I could bring a couple of friends with me."

"When are you going?"

"Next Thursday. You'd have to miss school on Friday."

"Oh, wouldn't that be too bad? Missing school?" Janelle laughed. "I'm sure my mom would let me. I've been extra good and helpful around the house because I was hoping Greg would ask me out, and I wanted to be on her good side when he did. I might as well use up my good credit now. Greg may never wake up and realize how ravishing I really am!"

Christy heard someone, probably Katie, laughing in the background. "I was going to invite Katie, too. Do you think she can go?"

"She's right here. I'll ask her."

Christy heard their muffled conversation in the background. When Janelle came back on the line, she said, "Katie can't go because of the game next Friday night."

"Oh, I forgot," Christy said. "That's too bad."

"But Brittany's here," Janelle added. "She said she'd love to go with us. Is that okay?"

"Sure," Christy said.

"Oh," Janelle cut back in. "Katie said we have to leave for the stadium in about half an hour, so hurry up and call me back if you want a ride."

"Okay. Thanks! Bye."

It was amazing how energetic Christy felt after that phone call, even though her mom said Christy couldn't go to the game. At this point it was that they had included her that mattered. She had so much to look forward to—church on Sunday, Palm Springs next weekend. Why did she doubt her new friends' loyalty? They invited her to the game, didn't they?

Christy woke up Sunday morning in a great mood. Slipping

her best blue dress over her head and adjusting the top, she thought back to when Aunt Marti bought it for her last summer. She hadn't worn it since the night Todd took her to the Debbie Stevens's concert. It made her feel pretty and sophisticated.

After carefully applying her makeup, she hung her head down and brushed and brushed her short, nutmeg-colored hair until it was full all around. Then, shielding her eyes, she quickly squirted on some spritz. One last look. One last dab of mascara.

She thought she heard a car pull in the driveway. Christy grabbed her purse and the Bible Todd and Tracy had given her and hurried to the front door.

"Be sure to take your key," Mom called through her parents' closed bedroom door. "We might run a few errands while you're gone."

"Okay. See you later. Bye."

David looked away from the TV as Christy swished past and said, "Where are you going?"

"Church. See you later."

Christy felt a little self-conscious on the way to church. Janelle and Katie kept commenting on her hair and her outfit and how nice she looked. The remarks made her feel uncomfortable in a good way. It was better than being ignored any day.

When they pulled into a huge parking lot, Christy asked in surprise, "Is this your church?"

"Yes. Why?" Janelle said.

"It's so huge!"

"Not really," Katie said. "What was your church like back in Ohio?"

"Wisconsin. And our church was, well, like a church. White with a steeple, and the little kids met in the basement. Our high school Sunday school class had about seven people in it—on a good Sunday."

"Get ready for a surprise, then!" Janelle said. "I think we have 250 in our high school group."

They walked briskly toward a building Janelle called the "Youth Facility." Christy held her breath as they entered a large room with seats set up like a movie theater. Four guys stood in the front of the room playing guitars while another played a keyboard. All the high-schoolers were sitting or standing around, talking above the volume of the upbeat music.

"You okay?" Janelle asked, looking at Christy's face.

"I've never been to a Sunday school like this before!" Christy said over the loud music.

"Come on, let's find a seat."

They found three seats together, and Christy sat on the end, looking around her blankly as Janelle and Katie continued their nonstop conversation. A pretty girl with flawless skin and perfect white teeth tapped Christy on the shoulder.

"Hi. Welcome!" she said brightly. "Would you mind filling this out for us so we can put you on our mailing list and let you know about upcoming activities?"

She smelled fresh, like baby powder.

Christy quickly filled out the small card with her name and address. The last line said, "Hobbies."

"What should I put?" Christy asked Janelle. "I don't have any hobbies."

"I know," said Janelle. "That's so dumb. Do you like to ski or swim or sew or anything like that?"

"Not really."

"I know!" said Katie with a mischievous twinkle in her eye. "Put down 'toilet papering.' "

"Yeah, right!" Christy said.

"No, do it! It'll be funny," Janelle urged.

Oh, well. The girl said they just needed it for their mailing list. So she wrote it down.

"Thanks," said the girl, who had patiently waited for Christy to fill out the card. "We're really glad to have you here visiting us. Hope you'll come again!"

"She's nice," Christy said.

"Who, Wendy?"

Christy nodded and looked toward Wendy. Her blond hair, pulled back in a French braid, looked as if gold threads had been carefully woven into it by the sun.

"Wendy's our model," Katie said. "She's so perfect. We all wish we could be like her by the time we're seniors."

"She's also Rick's girlfriend."

Christy's heart froze. The mention of Rick made her feel squeamish.

"They're not going together," Katie said bluntly.

"I heard they went out twice already, and she was at the game Friday night. They probably went out after the game, too."

"So they've gone out two, maybe three times, huh? I suppose in your opinion, Janelle, they're practically engaged."

"I didn't say that."

"But that's what you insinuated."

"Katie, I hate it when you use all your big words," Janelle said.

Christy ventured to disrupt their play-fight. "What's 'insinuate'?"

Katie looked at Janelle and then turned toward Christy, her shiny hair doing its little swishing fan motion. "It means, maybe that's not what Janelle said, but that's what she meant. It's the same as 'intimated.'"

"Intimated?" Christy questioned, scrunching up her nose.

Janelle and Katie looked at each other, and then they both burst into laughter. Christy couldn't tell if they were laughing at her or at each other or what. All her self-conscious feelings began to rise. She considered ducking out, finding the rest room, and hiding there for a while.

A guy in his late twenties with brown hair stepped to the microphone in the front of the room: "Good morning, everyone!" People started quieting down and finding their seats. The guy at the microphone ran through some quick announcements and then said, "We'd like to take a minute now and introduce our visitors."

Suddenly, Rick Doyle stepped up to the microphone. Tall and smiling, dressed in dark slacks and a white shirt, he held a few cards in his hand. He scanned the room for a second, and then, as if he found what he was looking for, his gaze stopped at Christy and stayed there as he spoke to the group.

"Okay, listen up everybody. We have four visitors this morning, and I want you guys to make them feel welcome. First one here is Christina Miller. Would you stand up, Christina?"

Christy froze in her seat. Her heart pounded. She couldn't move.

"Stand up," Katie urged, pulling her up by the arm.

"Come on," Janelle nudged. "Stand up!"

"She's kind of shy," Katie said loud enough for the whole room to hear.

Everyone turned and looked at her. With every ounce of nerve, Christy fought the panic that paralyzed her and stood, trembling. *Why didn't they tell me I was going to have to stand up and be introduced? I never would've filled out that card! And why is Rick the one doing the introductions?*

"Christina is a sophomore at Kelley High," Rick read from the card, "and it says here that her hobby is 'toilet papering.'"

The whole room burst into laughter.

"At least she admits it!" Rick said loudly into the microphone.

He was looking right at her and smiling broadly. "We're real glad to have you here, Christina."

Christy dropped to her seat and kept looking straight ahead, her teeth clenched, her face burning with embarrassment. Janelle and Katie giggled beside her as if they'd planned this little prank all along. Rick introduced the other three visitors.

Christy wanted to melt into her seat or somehow evaporate into the air. This had to be the most embarrassing moment of her entire life.

In a few minutes, the group was dismissed to go into separate classrooms. Christy kept her head down, staring at her feet, reluctantly following Janelle and Katie to their elective class on First Corinthians.

Suddenly, someone stood before her, blocking her exit. She looked up hesitantly, holding her breath. It was Rick!

"So," he said, smiling broadly, "your name is Christina." He stood there, tall and confident, completely overwhelming Christy. She could barely make her head nod and her mouth form a light smile.

"I'm Rick." He stuck out his hand to shake hers.

Christy forced her sweating palm into his strong grip. She tried to push the word "Hi" from her throat, but it wouldn't come.

Rick let go of her hand. "I've been telling everybody about the night you popped out of the bushes at my house. That was incredible. And then didn't I see you in the hall at school last week?"

Christy forced out a breathy laugh and nodded her head ever so slightly.

"Well, we'd better go to class," Rick suggested. "I think your friends went in here." Rick opened the door to a small classroom where about 35 chairs formed a half circle.

Janelle and Katie were both sitting in the back row, chatting briskly about something. They immediately stopped and stared wide-eyed when Rick held the door open for Christy and pointed to two empty seats for them in the front row. Christy noticed that Janelle and Katie weren't motioning for her to sit by them, and when someone took the seat next to Janelle, she didn't act as though she were trying to save it for Christy. Pulling together her courage and composure, she gracefully slipped into the seat in the front row where Rick was offering for her to sit beside him.

As the class began, Christy found it nearly impossible to pay attention to what the teacher was saying. She did manage to find the verses in her Bible that he referred to, but the letters looked blurred as Rick, who didn't have a Bible, looked on with her.

This is so stupid! What good is it to have my dreams come true if I'm too jittery to just relax and enjoy it?

She had done the same thing on a bike ride to Balboa Island with Todd last summer, and she had vowed she would never again space out when she was with a guy. Thinking of Todd brought a calm sensation over her.

Why am I even worried about what this guy thinks of me? What does that say about my feelings for Todd? Was that just a summer thing? Is Brittany right about moving on, since Todd is never going to write to me? Why am I thinking all these things right now? We're supposed to be studying the Bible!

Christy forced herself to listen and try to comprehend what the teacher was saying about the verse before her. She focused on the passage until she could read it: "Do not be misled: 'Bad company corrupts good character'" (1 Corinthians 15:33).

Someone raised a hand and asked, "I still think you should try to have friends that aren't Christians, because how else can you lead them to the Lord?"

"True, true," the teacher, an older man with thick glasses and black hair, answered. "But the key question is, are they bringing you down? In other words, are you having an influence on them, or are they having the greater influence on you?"

"Most of my friends aren't Christians," one of the guys said. "There are hardly any Christians at my school. And if you really want to know the truth, some of the girls I've gone out with from my school are, like, way more moral than some of the Christian girls I've dated."

"Okay, that's a valid point," the teacher said, standing up. He looked as if he were really getting into the discussion. "Let me give you something to think about. Is it okay for a committed Christian to get involved in an ongoing dating relationship with someone who's not a Christian?"

"How else are they going to come to the church and learn about God and everything?" one girl asked.

"I didn't say a one-time date, like bringing them to a church activity or group dating with a bunch of your church friends. I said an ongoing dating relationship. Going steady, or whatever you call it now. What do you think?"

Everyone hesitated to answer aloud, but Christy could hear them murmuring among themselves. She thought it was okay. As long as the Christian stayed strong. But she didn't say anything.

"Let me show you something," the teacher said. "Here are my feelings on 'missionary dating.' "

"Missionary dating?" one of the girls behind Christy echoed.

"Yes. You know, when you feel like you're a missionary called to go steady with all the cute unbelievers in Escondido."

Everyone chuckled.

"Rick, come up here. Stand beside my chair, will you? Go ahead. Just stand up here. Now, let's see . . . Katie! You come up here, too. Katie, you stand on top of my chair. That's right, right here. Okay now, Rick, you are 'Peter Pagan.' "

Everyone laughed. Christy smiled. Rick looked so self-confident and bold standing beside the chair with his arms folded across his chest.

"And Katie, you are 'Katie Christian.' "

Katie made a cute little curtsy, balancing gingerly on the chair, her bright green eyes flashing. Christy felt a tiny twinge of jealousy. But she knew she would have died if the teacher had called her up to stand next to Rick in front of the class.

"Now, Katie, you are a sold-out Christian. You have surrendered your life to Christ, and you are committed to living for Him and following Him obediently.

"Rick, I mean, Peter Pagan, you are clueless when it comes to things of the Lord. Not that you haven't heard the gospel. After all, you're a red-blooded American, right? But you haven't given your life to Christ, and so all you know is the way of the world and following after your own desires."

Rick posed with a toothy smile, raising his eyebrows and twirling an imaginary mustache like a villain in an old-time play.

"Katie, you are convinced that missionary dating is the only way to reach this guy, so you begin going out with him regularly."

"Oooo, Katie!" Janelle hooted as others laughed.

"So, Katie, you and Peter Pagan hold hands." Katie obeyed; her cheeks instantly turned a shade of red that almost clashed with her orangish-red hair.

"Katie, you are such a strong Christian," the teacher said, "that you are going to influence Peter Pagan for good. You're going to bring him to God. Go ahead. You pull Peter up to the chair where you stand. Go ahead, pull harder."

Katie yanked and tugged, but Rick barely moved.

"Not so easy, is it? Now, Peter Pagan, try your influence on Katie. You bring her down to your level."

With one quick tug, Katie toppled off the chair and literally fell into Rick's arms. His quick reflexes allowed him to catch her with a solid thud, before both of them crashed to the floor.

The classroom filled with laughter as Katie pulled away from Rick's chest.

With a crimson face, she asked the teacher, "May I sit down now, or do you want me to go lie down in front of a train or something?"

"Thanks, Katie. I knew you'd be a good sport. You can sit down now."

Rick and Katie both returned to their chairs as the teacher drove home his point. "What do you think? Was it easier for Katie Christian to pull her boyfriend up to her level, or was it easier for Peter Pagan to pull her down to his level?"

There was a pause. No one needed to answer aloud. It was obvious that everyone got the point.

"This verse makes it very clear. Let's read it again, 'Do not be misled: "Bad company corrupts good character." ' If you don't remember anything else from this chapter, remember this verse. Bad friends could ruin your whole life. Be wise when it comes to choosing your friends. You set the standard. You be the one who stands strong. Don't be a follower."

The teacher paced the floor in front of the class for a brief moment, pulling up his next thoughts. "And for all of you who think God has called you to a life of missionary dating, well, don't be misled. I should bring my sister in here next week. She could tell you all about her results of missionary dating. She ended up marrying the guy, and he still isn't saved. They've been married 12 years and have three kids, and my sister is the loneliest person I know." He looked at his watch and then looked up, showing his feelings of pain for his sister by the pinched look on his face.

"That's all for this week. We'll finish chapter 15 of First Corinthians next week. Any of you who want a jump-start on this, read from verse 35 to the end of the chapter. Next week we're going to talk about the resurrection."

Rick stood and began talking to some of the guys beside him, who were teasing him, calling him Peter Pagan. He wasn't exactly ignoring Christy, but he wasn't including her in the conversation either. She hung around for a few minutes until Janelle and Katie walked by close enough for her to slip into the herd that moved with them. All the other girls were teasing Katie and talking about the chair demonstration.

The group of seven girls all sat together in the sanctuary. Right before the service began, Rick walked past the row where Christy sat. The girls watched him go up two rows and slide past four people to an empty seat by Wendy. Wendy, the perfect girl. It appeared that she had saved the seat for him.

"See," Janelle whispered around Christy to Katie, who was sitting on her other side. "I told you they were going together."

"So what?" Katie answered in a singsong voice. "He held hands with me in public!"

The two girls laughed quietly at Katie's comment, and Christy sat perfectly still between them, something bothering her. *Why did Janelle tell Brittany that Rick was interested in me if Janelle was so sure that Wendy and Rick were going together?*

She was finding it hard to understand her new friends. It still bothered Christy that they hadn't saved a seat for her in the classroom, but she didn't know how to tell them it had bothered her. What bothered her more was that Brittany had fed her all this information about Rick asking about her and now it didn't seem to be making sense.

Christy tried hard to remember all the things Brittany had said about Rick being intrigued with her. Every time Brittany had said her source of information had been Janelle. So, why wasn't Janelle telling Christy these things? All Janelle seemed convinced of was that Wendy and Rick were dating.

Christy stood at the appropriate times in the service and sang the words to the songs, but her mind played laser tag with all the unanswered questions about Rick and what Brittany had said.

When the sermon began, Christy jotted a note to Janelle on the back of her bulletin: *Janelle, did you tell Brittany that Rick wanted to meet me?*

Janelle read it and gave Christy a look that said, "Oh, come on! You've got to be kidding!" She wrote, *No. Why?*

Brit said you'd talked to him a couple of times and that he knew you had the slumber party. He wanted to know who I was. Is that true?

Janelle discreetly read the note and then gave Christy a look that said, "I'm sorry, but no," and gently shook her dark, curly hair.

Christy bit her lower lip and blinked quickly before any tears could form. Why did Brittany lie to her? Why would she make up all that stuff? Was it just so Christy would be convinced she needed to lose weight, like Brittany was?

Janelle, noticing the look on Christy's face, quickly scribbled another note on the front side of the bulletin: *Don't worry about it. It looks as though you managed to meet Rick fine, all by yourself. You didn't need Brit to arrange it for you.*

Christy smiled a "thank you" to Janelle, but her heart still felt squashed. She tried to pay attention to the sermon, but her eyes kept darting over to the back of Rick's head. His curly, brown hair was tilted only a few inches from Wendy's gold-spun French braid. They even looked good together from the back.

Soon the congregation stood to sing the last song and then be dismissed. Katie, Janelle, and Christy stood around talking with some other girls. Rick huddled with some guys only a few feet away.

"Come on," Rick said to the other guys, "let's ask them." He and the guys moved toward the group where Christy stood.

"You girls want to go out for pizza with us?" Rick asked.

"Sure," said Katie. "Who else is going?"

Rick recited a list of names with Wendy's name appearing at the top of the list.

"I can't," Janelle said. "We're going to see my grandma."

"How about you?" Rick said, looking at Christy.

"I guess not. I came with Janelle."

"I'll give you a ride home afterward," Rick offered.

Christy wasn't sure. Then she remembered her mother telling her to take her key because they might run errands. *They're probably not even home,* Christy thought. She looked up at Rick. "Sure, that would be okay."

"It would be more than okay," Janelle said in a muffled tone behind Christy's back. Aloud she said, "Have fun."

CHAPTER EIGHT

Slow Down, Honey

Christy and Katie followed the guys to the parking lot as the group headed out for pizza. Squished into the backseat of Rick's cherry red Mustang, Christy and Katie kept bumping knees. A guy Christy hadn't met sat in the front seat.

"Your car is in great shape," Katie said as Rick pulled out of the driveway. "What year is it?"

"'68. Used to be my mom's. My parents had it up on blocks in the garage for a long time. That's why it's still in good shape. You drive yet, Katie?"

"No."

"How about you, Christina?"

"No."

"Then you must be under 16," he said, looking at them in the rearview mirror.

"We're both 15 and proud of it," Katie said.

"Just babies," the guy next to Rick said.

Katie slugged the guy in the arm. "Hey! Fifteen is a very nice age, thank you very much."

Katie and the guy exchanged quick, rude little comments all the way to the pizza place. Christy sat back and watched, feeling excited and nervous. Twice she caught Rick looking at her in the rearview mirror. *I wonder what he's thinking?*

Rick parked the Mustang next to Wendy's car and held the seat forward as Christy tried to step out gracefully. She feared she might do something klutzy, like trip or tear her dress. But nothing happened. Maybe her awkward days were over. Maybe she was becoming as mature as she felt in this blue dress.

Rick walked beside her and held open one of the double doors of the restaurant. "After you, miss," he said, bowing playfully. "Nice dress," he added.

"Thanks," Christy said, looking up at him bravely, wondering if he would sit by her. He was so tall that he actually made her feel petite. No guy had ever made her feel petite before. Just as she slid beneath his arm, which was propping the door open, he leaned forward and said softly into the back of her head, "You're not going to run away this time, are you?"

Christy blushed and turned to look at him, smiling. He was so good-looking.

"No, not this time," she said softly.

"Good." Rick's smile melted Christy's heart. He slid past her, leading the way to the counter where a group of eight of them stood, deciding on what kinds of toppings to order on their pizzas.

"I've got only five dollars," Christy said quietly to Katie. "Who should I give it to?"

"You've got more than I do. Here, I'll take it." Katie moved up beside Rick and flashed a bright smile. "Oh, Peter Pagan!" she said loudly. "Here's nine dollars for Christy and me. And we want Coke if you're going to order by the pitcher." Katie turned to get Christy's attention. "You like Coke, don't you?"

Christy nodded as her mind flashed back to a searing memory of the party she had gone to in Newport Beach last summer. She had been left all alone to try and fit in. She had asked for something to drink, "some Coke." To her horror, one of the surfers thought she was asking for cocaine and sent her upstairs to the bedroom where a small group sat around smoking dope. She had run from the house, feeling like a baby. But that's when Todd caught up with her, and they had sat together on the jetty, watching the sunset and talking.

I'm glad I ran out the door that time. But I'm not running away anymore, Christy thought. *Not from Rick, not from anything.*

After ordering the pizzas, the group moved to the back room. Christy sat at the same booth as Katie, and to her delight, Rick moved briskly past another guy and slid onto the red vinyl seat, next to Christy.

Wendy and her friends sat in their own separate booth across the way. It looked as though two of the guys were competing for Wendy's attention.

She must not be Rick's girlfriend! Christy thought triumphantly. *And he's sitting next to me!* Feeling flirty and fun-loving, Christy laughed at everything Rick said.

But it was Katie who kept the conversation rolling, and the guys loved her. She had a fresh, tomboyish way about her that made everyone feel comfortable around her.

Christy didn't say much. All the others were talking so quickly that she couldn't squeeze much in. Plus, it seemed that whenever she thought of something clever, the group had already passed that particular subject.

Katie was quick. She had unbelievably fast comebacks. Christy wished Katie could go to Palm Springs with them next weekend.

Once the hot pizza, covered with simmering pepperoni, arrived, Christy ate only one piece; Katie had several, and the guys devoured the rest. Rick must have eaten at least 10 pieces.

"I think Christy and I should get a refund," Katie said, eyeing the emptied pans before them. "We didn't get our nine dollars' worth. We merely made a contribution to support you guys' pizza habit."

"Let me be the first to thank you," one of the guys said. "I was beginning to have pepperoni withdrawal. You saved me, Katie Christian!"

"Oh, great! Just when I was getting used to Katie Cougar!"

"Here," Rick offered, pitching her a quarter, "here's your refund."

Another guy tossed a quarter in the center of the table. "Hey, remember Hume Lake?" he asked. "Time to defend your title, Katie. Come on, guys! The quarter game!"

"Do you know how to play this?" Rick asked Christy.

"No."

"We have two quarters that we pass under the table. Katie's going to stand at the end of the booth watching, and when she says stop, we put our fists on the top of the table."

"Like this," the other guys said, putting the thumb side of their fists up and pounding on the table like a drum.

"Then Katie says stop again, and we have to put our hands flat on the table. See, if you have one of the quarters, you try to keep it from being seen or heard. Then Katie has to guess which two hands have the quarters."

"Got it?" Katie asked.

"I think so," Christy said, scooting up to the edge of the table. "Let's practice."

Katie stood at the front of the booth. "Ready? Go!"

Christy placed her hands on top of her knees under the table, waiting for the quarter to be passed to her. All the guys were moving their arms, and she couldn't tell who was passing the quarters.

Suddenly, the guy on her right pressed a quarter into her open palm. Christy quickly passed it to her left hand, then moved her hand toward Rick, to pass it on to him. At the same moment that she touched Rick's hand, ready to give him the quarter, he pushed the other quarter into her hand.

"Stop," Katie yelled, and 10 fists went up on the table. Christy squeezed her hand tightly as she pounded the table with the others.

"Stop."

All the guys laid their hands flat. Christy fumbled a bit, trying to get her fingers out and the quarters to lie flat. It didn't work. One quarter stuck out through her middle fingers, and the other one slid off the table and onto the floor.

Christy burst into laughter, and Katie said, "Now, let me guess. Could it be Christy?"

"That was a trial run," Rick said quickly. "Practice only. It doesn't count."

"Okay," Katie said, retrieving the quarter and placing it on the table. "This one counts for real. Okay, guys?" Her bright jade eyes scanned each player as the quarters made their rounds.

"Stop."

They pounded the table.

"Stop."

All fists lay flat. Katie picked two hands, but neither had the quarters. Rick had one of them, and he laughed when Christy said, "That's no fair! Your hand is twice the size of mine."

"Here," Rick said, poking his hand into his pocket. He pulled out a dime and handed it to Christy. "Is this more your size?"

They all laughed.

"Come on," Katie said. "Quarters only. Let's get going."

They played round after round, and Christy spent most of the time as the "spotter" since she got caught nearly every time she had the quarter. She didn't mind. She was having a great time.

"I've got to get going," one of the guys said.

Christy didn't want to leave. This was too much fun. She wanted to sit next to Rick and laugh and have a good time all afternoon. But everyone else got up and walked out to the parking lot.

Christy slipped into the backseat with Katie again, and Rick asked, "You guys going to church tonight?"

"I don't know," Christy answered. She wasn't sure her parents would let her, and she had some homework she hadn't done yet.

"I probably am," Katie answered, "but I don't think you were asking me, were you?"

Rick didn't answer. He had turned on the radio, and the guy in the front seat began drumming the dashboard in time with the music.

When Rick pulled into Christy's driveway, she was surprised to see the car there. She thought her family would still be out shopping. Their car looked so old and junky compared with Rick's polished red Mustang.

"Thanks for the ride, Rick," Christy said when she slipped out.

"Anytime," he returned.

"I'll see you guys later." Christy waved good-bye and swung open the front door, her heart singing.

"Where have you been?" Christy's mom jumped up from the couch.

"At church. I told you I was going to church."

"Church? From 8:30 in the morning until 2:30 in the afternoon? You've been at church this whole time?"

"No, I mean yes, I mean . . ." Her dad walked in from the back of the house, and Christy caught her breath. "I was at church until noon, and then I went out to lunch."

"You didn't ask us if you could go out to lunch."

"I didn't know until after church."

"You should have called, Christy," her dad said firmly. "We've been worried sick. We had absolutely no idea where you were. We didn't even remember what church you were going to."

"I thought you were going to run errands. I didn't call because I didn't think you'd be home," Christy said.

"We did run errands," Mom said. "But we got back before noon. We had no idea where you were."

David burst through the front door. "Who was that guy in the red car, Christy? Did you see his car, Dad? I tried to race him to the corner on my bike, but he beat me."

Dad's eyebrows rose as he looked his daughter in the eye. "You went out to lunch with a young man?"

"Yes, well, sort of. A bunch of us went, guys and girls, all from church. Rick just gave me a ride home. Two other people were in the car. Katie was in the car." Christy talked fast, afraid that she was in big trouble.

"What happened to Janelle?" Mom asked, crossing her arms in front of her.

"Janelle had to go home after church, but Katie and I went to lunch with everybody because Rick offered to give us a ride."

"Why didn't you come home when Janelle did?" Mom asked.

"I-I don't know. I guess I wanted to go out to lunch with everybody."

Christy's dad looked at her mom, then they both looked at Christy.

"Listen carefully, young lady," Dad said in his sternest voice. "I'm sure you didn't mean to worry us like this, but you should have used better judgment. You should have come home with Janelle or at least called and asked about going out to lunch. You're not allowed to date yet, and that includes accepting rides with people we've never met—especially teenage guys. Actually, I don't want you riding in a car with a bunch of teenagers at all. Is that understood?"

"Yes, I'm sorry," Christy said. It was the first time she'd ever heard him actually say she wasn't allowed to date. The question had never come up when they lived in Wisconsin. "I didn't think it would be a problem since it was with a bunch of people from church."

His expression softened. "Well, too many kids don't think, and that's the problem."

"You've got to be more responsible, Christy," her mom said, sitting back down on the couch. "You can't take off for hours without us knowing where you are. Don't you see?"

"Yes, I see," Christy said. She didn't like this thick, heavy, sick feeling she always got in the pit of her stomach whenever her parents "counseled" her like this. She always ended up feeling miserable and foolish for not thinking things through ahead of time. She turned to go to her room.

"One more thing," her dad added. "Where in the world did you get that dress?"

"From Aunt Marti. She bought it for me in San Francisco."

Her dad shook his head. "You kids always want to jump ahead and try to look older than you are—try to use up your youth. Don't you realize that once it's gone you can never get it back?"

He stepped closer to Christy, his eyes looked misty. "Slow down, honey," he said in a tender, hoarse voice. "Just slow down, will you?"

Her father's words plagued her all week long. At home, walking down the hall at school, playing volleyball in P.E. class—everywhere she went she could hear him saying, "Slow down, honey."

After about three days of sloshing that phrase around in her brain, she wrote in her diary:

The thing is, I'm not really trying to grow up too fast. All these things are happening to me, and I'm just trying to keep up with them. I think it would be different if I were rebelling or something. But I'm trying to do the right thing. Well, at least most of the time.

I'm sure Dad's right, that I don't always think things through. But he doesn't know all the good choices I've made, or all the stuff I've already said no to.

I've been trying to figure out what God wants me to do. I think He wants me to try really hard to do the right thing and say no to everything that looks like it wouldn't be good for me.

No, no, no, no. There, my daily practice in saying no.

CHAPTER NINE

Fun, Fun, Fun

The week zoomed by. Christy's mom got the job at Mr. Taylor's real estate office. David fell off his bike and had to get four stitches in his chin. Christy's dad planted some bushes and fixed the screen door.

Although Christy scanned the halls every day for Rick, she never saw him. By Thursday afternoon, she hardly gave him a thought. She was going to Palm Springs with her friends, and the three of them were brimming with excitement.

"You girls all ready to go?" Uncle Bob asked as he tightened down a suitcase on the trunk rack of his Mercedes convertible. The luggage for the five of them had been more than the trunk of his car could handle.

He checked his pockets for his keys and said, "Oh, here, Christy. A couple of letters for you. The one I told you about over the phone last week," he said, handing her an envelope addressed in Paula's handwriting. "And here's another one that came yesterday."

For one hopeful moment, Christy thought, *Todd! He finally wrote to me!*

She reached for the envelope and looked at the return address. It was from Tracy. Tracy, the girl from the beach whom

Christy had tried so hard to not like. But sweet Tracy had always been kind to Christy. *Why would Tracy be writing to me? She and Todd are close friends. Maybe there's some news about Todd.*

The three girls settled snugly in the backseat of the comfortable car. Aunt Marti's perfume filled the air around them since Bob had left the top up on the car. With one last wave to Christy's mom and a dejected-looking David, they were on their way.

While Janelle and Brittany discussed different kinds of perms with Aunt Marti, Christy quietly read her letter from Paula. Paula wrote with strong emotion, saying how much she missed Christy and that she couldn't wait until June, when she would come out to California. She said she would never find another friend like Christy. Her birthday party this Saturday night would be the first time since kindergarten that Christy had missed celebrating with Paula.

Christy faced the window. The dry scenery rolled past as she blinked back the tears. *I wish you were here now, Paula. I wish you were going to Palm Springs with us. I miss you, too.*

Christy realized that her relationship with Paula had become something different. Still friends, still close, even though apart. Still a part of each other's lives. Yet they had definitely stepped into a different season of their friendship. What really hurt was that Paula didn't understand Christy's summer promise. She didn't see that to have a relationship with Jesus, you must first make a commitment to Him. *It took me awhile to understand it, Paula. I'll keep praying for you the way Todd and Tracy prayed for me.*

She tucked Paula's letter into the side pocket of her purse and then quickly scanned Tracy's note card. It was short and sweet, just like Tracy.

Dear Christy,
    I read this verse today, and I thought about you, so I decided to send it your way:

"The Lord himself goes before you and will be with you; he will never leave you nor forsake you. Do not be afraid; do not be discouraged" (Deuteronomy 31:8).

I hope everything is going well for you and that you're making lots of friends at your new school. Let us know whenever you're up here at the beach again. We all miss you.

Love,
Tracy

Of all the girls Christy had met at the beach last summer, Tracy was the friendliest. She had gone out of her way more than once to be kind to Christy.

I'd like to be more like Tracy, Christy thought. *She thinks about her friends and their needs more than she thinks of herself.*

"Do you girls mind listening to one of my oldie-moldy favorites?" Bob asked. Before they answered, he popped a CD into the stereo and cranked it up.

"Really, Robert!" Marti scolded. "Must you turn it up so loud?"

Janelle and Brittany were already singing along. Bob respectfully turned it down a bit and slipped his sunglasses up on top of his head, looking his wife in the eye. "Come on, babe! Tell me this doesn't bring back memories?"

She smiled and reached across the seat, giving his arm a squeeze. "You haven't changed a bit, Bobby. Always Mr. Fun, Fun, Fun . . ."

Janelle knew the words to every song. "My brothers have this CD. I love it!"

Bob really got into it, drumming on the steering wheel, bopping his head back and forth. "Think your hair can take the breeze if I put the top down?" he asked Marti.

"Yes! Let's put the top down!" Janelle said enthusiastically.

"Oh, no, dear. I don't have a scarf with me. I'd prefer you left it up. Besides, the air conditioning feels so refreshing."

"What are we going to do tonight?" Christy asked sometime later, after the song fest died down.

"We'll go straight to the hotel and check in; then we'll change and go out for dinner," Marti announced.

Aunt Marti, you would have made a great cruise director on a luxury liner, Christy thought with a smile.

"You girls like Italian or Chinese?" Bob asked, turning off the stereo.

"What?" Janelle asked. "Guys or food?"

Bob laughed. "Either."

"Both!" Janelle giggled.

"I see I've met my match in your friend, Christy," Bob said, pulling off the freeway onto a long road that appeared to be heading straight for a high range of mountains. The car traveled in the shade now; everything looked different—purple-tinted.

"How much farther?" Christy asked.

"A few miles. You can almost see the aerial tramway from here."

"What's that?"

"The Palm Springs tram runs from the desert floor to the top of Mount San Jacinto there. It's about 8,000 feet up, and in the winter it's covered with snow."

Bob bent his head forward, looking out the windshield. "I've got a great story about that mountain. A few years ago I went up in November with some of my golf buddies to go hiking. When we got on the tram, it was cloudy; but by the time we got to the top, it was freezing. After we ate lunch at the restaurant up there, we were all set to go on our hike when it started snowing. Crazy part was, I got sunburned golfing the day before!"

"You girls would enjoy going up on the tram, wouldn't you?

You could take them on Saturday, couldn't you, Bob?" Marti said.

"Sounds like a plan. Or we could take a ride in a hot air balloon."

"Really?" Christy squealed.

"That's something I've always wanted to do!" Brittany said.

"That'd be hot!" chimed in Janelle. "Get it? Hot? Hot air balloon?"

"We get it, Janelle," Christy said. "That's why we're not laughing."

How fun! Christy thought. *I always wanted to ride in a hot air balloon.* She hummed to herself the rest of the way while the others kept discussing their plans. "And we'll have fun, fun, fun . . ."

"Here we are," Bob said as they drove down a street lined with shops, restaurants, and office buildings. "Palm Canyon Drive."

Christy wasn't impressed. After all she had heard about Palm Springs, she expected some wonderfully glamorous, fancy town. The shops and everything looked nice but not spectacular.

Bob pulled into a hotel parking lot and stopped under a huge portico supported by white pillars. A valet opened the door, and a rush of hot desert wind engulfed them. The valet offered his hand to each of the girls as he helped them out of the car. Christy loved being pampered like this.

Another uniformed man piled all their luggage onto a cart and followed them to the reservations desk.

"Look at that fountain!" Janelle gasped when they entered the spacious lobby.

Christy thought the lobby, with its adobe-style decor looked like a movie set. It was so grand and different from anything she'd ever seen before. The floor was a pinkish-clay color, and the walls were a white tile with a lot of Native American rugs hanging on them. There was a lot of open space and light. The hallways were decorated with big clay pots holding tall cacti.

"Look," Janelle said, pressing one of the stickers on a cactus. "They're fake." The pointed needle sticker that appeared so dangerous bent beneath Janelle's touch like an overcooked spaghetti noodle.

They were led down the wide hallway, and Christy thought, *This is like a movie. It's not real, but it's so fun! I love playing the part of the spoiled little rich girl.*

"I trust you'll be pleased with your rooms," the bellhop said, opening the door to the girls' suite.

Their eyes swept the spacious room. It had a sliding glass door opening onto the pool and deck. The bedspreads and curtains had the mosaic look of Native American rugs, only done in softer colors. On the walls hung several pictures of blooming cacti and desert wildflowers. Christy decided she liked the old-fashioned, Victorian look of the St. Francis in San Francisco better.

"This is totally hot!" Janelle said.

"Then you may wish to adjust the thermostat over there," the bellhop said with a straight face, pointing to the wall by the bathroom.

The three girls looked at each other and burst into laughter.

Bob handed the attendant some money and said, "They're my fan club. I take them with me wherever I go. Keeps me young."

"Now you girls get yourselves situated," Aunt Marti directed. "Our room is right next door. Shall we leave for dinner in, say, half an hour?"

"Sure."

"Sounds good to me."

The three of them quickly unpacked, chattering and laughing as Janelle explored the room, trying out every light switch and faucet and examining the complimentary basket filled with soap, shampoo, conditioner, lotion, and a shower cap.

"How does it look?" Janelle asked, stepping out of the bath-room with the shower cap over her head. "Should I wear it to dinner tonight in case it rains?"

"Quite stunning!" Christy said. "It goes so well with your ten-nis shoes."

They all laughed, and Brittany asked what they were going to wear to dinner.

"I didn't even bring a dress," Christy moaned. "I just didn't think of it when I packed last night."

"I brought a couple," Brittany said. "You can wear one of mine."

Christy chose a turquoise knit dress of Brittany's and slipped into the bathroom to put it on. She couldn't get it over her hips. Jerking open the bathroom door, she hollered out, "What size is this thing?"

"A 3. Why?" Brittany said. "What size do you wear?"

"Not a 3, that's for sure." Christy tossed it back at Brittany.

"Here," Janelle said. "I brought a dress and a skirt. Do you want to wear one of mine?"

"Throw me the skirt. I've got a couple of T-shirts. I'm sure I can find one to wear with it." Christy zipped the skirt up with no problem.

"A 3," she muttered to herself. "Nobody wears a 3. A size 5, maybe, but not a 3."

The girls quickly put on their makeup and did their hair.

"You should use more eyeliner," Brittany told Christy. "Try this one," she said, handing Christy a container. "It's Plum Pas-sion. It would look good on you."

"Purple?" Christy exclaimed. "I don't know . . ."

"Here, I'll do it," Janelle said, and she and Brittany both went to work on Christy.

When they stepped away and Christy saw her image in the mirror, her first reaction was, "Yuck!" But she didn't want to hurt her friends' feelings as they admired their handiwork. Her eyes looked squinty with the thick mascara and heavy liner. She felt ridiculous. Like a toddler with Mommy's makeup on.

Then someone knocked on the door, and it was too late to change anything. Uncle Bob, dressed in a tan sports coat and navy blue slacks, whistled through his front teeth, "Wowie ka-zowie! You gals look great. We'd better get out of here, though. It smells like a perfume bomb just exploded in your room!"

They laughed and met Marti in the hallway. Christy had to admit, her aunt was a classy woman. She always looked just right for the occasion. Tonight her soft cream-colored silk dress shimmered in the light, and her diamond necklace and earrings sparkled brightly.

"Christy," Marti said, eyeing her makeup, short skirt, and sandaled feet, "I don't suppose you brought your blue dress with you, dear. You know, the one I bought you this summer at Macy's."

"I didn't think to bring it." Actually, after her dad's comments over the dress last Sunday, she had stuck it in the back of her closet and decide to leave it there until she was at least 18.

"Is that the only skirt you brought?" Marti prodded.

"Actually, it's Janelle's. I packed in such a hurry, I didn't think to bring anything really nice."

"Well, we plan to do some shopping tomorrow, anyway. Now we'll know what to look for first."

Christy shrank into the backseat of the car as the other two girls, in their crisp, perfect-for-the-occasion dresses, chatted away. Christy hated it when her aunt made her feel this way: scruffy, like a well-used rag doll. It was bad enough last summer, but now, in front of her friends, it was even worse.

When no one was looking, Christy licked the waxy-tasting lip-stick off her lips and ran a finger across each eyelid, wiping off the Plum Passion as best she could.

At the dimly lit Italian restaurant, they went over the exten-sive menu, asking Bob what everything was. On her uncle's rec-ommendation, Christy ordered the fettuccine. It sounded so ex-otic, but when the waiter set it in front of her, she thought, *This looks like squished, milky spaghetti.* That's kind of how it tasted to Christy's unsophisticated tastebuds, too.

A man in a tuxedo playing a violin stepped up to their table. Uncle Bob asked him to play some song with an Italian title that Christy had never heard of.

The musician smiled and nodded. Then, tucking the violin under his chin, he began to play. Slowly at first, then vigorously, he pulled the bow back and forth, putting his whole heart into it. Christy found herself holding her breath on the last few high notes as if she were squeezing them out of her lungs along with the musician. He ended as dramatically as he had begun and then drew his violin under his arm and bowed low.

"Bravo!" said Marti.

"Molto bello!" exclaimed Bob and slipped the artist what Christy thought looked like a $20 bill.

The man smiled and nodded; then taking Marti's hand, he kissed it. He moved to Janelle and did the same thing. She giggled and looked at Christy, who was next in line.

Christy thought it was a little embarrassing but very exciting at the same time. The musician barely brushed his lips across the top of her hand. She turned to see how Brittany would react to the gracious gesture, but Brittany was gone.

"She probably went to the bathroom," Janelle suggested.

In the 10 minutes that followed, Christy sloshed the fettuc-cine around on her plate and ended up eating another piece of garlic bread before deciding she was full.

"Do you suppose your friend is all right?" Marti asked.

"I'll go check on her," Christy offered.

"I'll go with you," Janelle said. As they walked away from the table, Janelle said softly, "She's probably throwing up. She's on this weird diet. I think she's too skinny."

"I know," Christy agreed. "She told me she takes her mom's diet pills."

Suddenly, Christy remembered the prescription bottle of diet pills Brittany had given her. She still had them in her purse, which was back at the table. *I've got to throw those things away,* she thought.

They found Brittany standing by the sink, combing her hair.

"I think I'm going to try another brand of hair spray," Brittany said. "The one I use now is drying my hair out too much."

Christy noticed a clump of hair in the sink. Brittany squirted her wrists with perfume and asked, "Is everyone else finished?"

"Almost," Christy said. "We came to check on you. You okay?"

"Of course." Brittany laughed nervously. "I'm ready for dessert!"

"Brittany," Janelle sounded like a parent, "you didn't just throw up, did you?"

Brittany lowered her voice and raised her eyebrows, looking innocent. "Of course not! Why do you ask?"

"Brittany! Tell me the truth. Are you done with your diet or are you still taking laxatives and stuff?"

"No, I'm not on a diet anymore, honest. I was only saying that dessert sounds good to me tonight."

Christy couldn't tell if she was lying or not.

Janelle seemed convinced. "I think we'd better get back. They're probably ready to go."

Instead of returning to the hotel, Marti suggested they park the car and do some window-shopping. A wonderfully warm desert breeze twirled around them as they strolled past brightly lit window displays. Janelle came up with all kinds of jokes about the things they spotted in the windows, practical necessities like black leather miniskirts and stainless-steel pasta makers.

She still had them laughing when they got back to the hotel. Christy pulled the key to their room out of her purse and thanked Uncle Bob for the fun evening and good dinner.

"My pleasure, ladies," he said. "I've got an 8:00 tee-off, so I'll probably grab a donut in the coffee shop. Maybe you girls would like to sleep in and have your breakfast out by the pool. They have a buffet brunch, don't they, Marti?"

"I think it's only on Saturday and Sunday."

"Well, if you girls get hungry at anytime, give room service a call," Bob said. "We'll see you sometime tomorrow, then. Good night."

"Sweet dreams!" Marti said.

The three of them changed into their nightshirts, and Janelle said, "I'm too hyper to just watch TV. Let's put our bathing suits on and go swimming!"

"I don't think we can," Christy said. "Doesn't the pool close at 10:00?"

"Maybe if we're real quiet, they won't know we're in there," Janelle said with a giggle.

"Oh, right!" Christy said. "Three girls jumping in the pool. That's going to be real quiet."

"Then let's go walk around the lobby," Janelle said.

"In our pajamas?" Christy asked.

Janelle kept trying to convince them to think of something fun to do, and Christy kept coming up with excuses of why they couldn't do any of Janelle's crazy ideas. To Christy's relief, something Brittany said prompted Janelle to start asking Brittany questions about Kurt.

Propping pillows against the headboard, Janelle quizzed Brittany. "I saw you talking with Kurt last week after school. Are you going to start going out with him again?"

"Are you kidding? I was telling him to get lost. He turns my stomach. What about you and Greg?" Brittany asked Janelle. "What's happening with him?"

"Not much. He did talk to me a couple of times last week. But he only flirts with me when there aren't any junior or senior girls around. I like him, but he almost scares me, you know what I mean?"

"He scares you?" Christy asked.

"It's like he's always a step ahead of me. I look at him, and I can't figure out what he's thinking. He's very mysterious and untouchable. I like that, but it also scares me. And speaking of untouchable guys, Christy, do you have any updates on Rick?"

Christy didn't say anything. She looked at Brittany for her reaction. Brittany looked her usual cool self. Christy decided now was the time to get everything out in the open about what Brittany had been telling her about Rick.

"Brittany, why did you say that Rick was interested in meeting me and that Janelle was giving you all the inside information?"

"That's right," Janelle joined in. "I heard you were saying some stuff about Rick that I never said. I want to know where I got all this detailed information that I supposedly passed on to you. Rick never asked about my slumber party or who Christy was."

Brittany sat perfectly still on the bed, her legs crossed under her. Her facial expression didn't change, but it seemed to Christy that Brittany's mind was spinning behind those steady eyes, trying to come up with the right answer.

Brittany jumped up from the bed. "Oh no! I think I left my curling iron on!" Sprinting into the bathroom, she closed the door.

"Oh, now that was convenient," Janelle said. "Why can't she just admit she's wrong and move on from there?"

"Should we go check on her?" Christy asked.

"No. She has to come out eventually. Sometimes she's a real case," Janelle said.

"She has some problems," Christy said, keeping her voice low. "We have to try to be fair. You know about her parents splitting up. Her dad is never home. I feel sorry for her. I think we should try to help her."

"I guess you're right. I should be more understanding. But why did she make up all that stuff about Rick?"

"I don't know." Christy shrugged and glanced over at the closed bathroom door. "There's no point in even talking about Rick. You were the one who said you thought Rick was going with Wendy."

"I don't know. I thought they were, but I guess he's the kind of guy that likes to play the field. He's a sweet talker, if you know what I mean. He can get any girl he wants, and he knows it. I guess nobody really knows what's going on inside the head of Rick Doyle." Janelle stretched out and made herself more comfortable with a pillow stuffed under her arm. "What about that guy you met last summer?"

"Todd?"

"Whatever happened to him?"

Christy took a deep breath. "I have no idea. The little sweetheart hasn't written me at all. I've sent him at least five letters. Somehow, I don't feel like it's over, though. I keep hoping I'll see him again someday."

"He sounded like the perfect dream guy."

Christy glanced up at the painting on the wall behind the bed and smiled. "He is. Todd is one of a kind. I'll never forget him." Her eyes misted over with tears, and as she blinked, all the wildflowers in the painting began to run together in a swirl of smeared pastels.

"There's nothing wrong with liking two guys at the same time, Christy. Or a whole bunch of guys, for that matter," Janelle said. "My mom says this is the time of our lives when we should go for as much attention as we can get. We should be the ones who decide whom we go out with and not wait around for the guys to decide if they're interested in us."

Christy blinked back the tears. "That could be, but it sure helps if at least one of those guys likes you back."

Janelle laughed. "Well said, Christy, well said. Now, if only Greg would ask me out and Rick would ask you out, then we could go on a double date!"

"Oh, right. Like that would ever happen."

"It could happen. Like for homecoming next weekend." Janelle's eyes took on their exotic glimmer. "Wouldn't that be fun?"

Christy was noticing that "fun" seemed to be Janelle's favorite word or at least her motivation for most of her decisions.

The bathroom door opened, and Brittany walked out, cool and composed. "Is anybody hungry besides me?" She opened the room service menu on the dresser and began reading the list.

Christy and Janelle exchanged wary looks, and Christy wondered if they should say anything to Brittany.

"A hot fudge sundae—$9.50!" Brittany squawked. "And look at this: soft drinks—$4.50! What a rip-off!"

"I don't think I could order anything with a clear conscience, knowing your uncle had to pay for it," Janelle said.

"He doesn't mind," Christy said. "Money doesn't mean the same thing to him that it does to my family."

"Hey, you guys, we still haven't done anything fun tonight. Don't you just feel like doing something wild?" Janelle asked.

"Like what?" Christy asked cautiously.

"I don't know. Like running up and down the hallway."

"I think I saw some vending machines at the end of the hallway," Brittany said. "Let's go and get a candy bar and a soda. It'll be cheaper than ordering from room service."

"I don't know if we should," Christy hesitated.

"Oh, come on! It'll be fun." Janelle was already standing up, ready to go.

"Should we go like this? In our nightshirts?" Brittany asked.

"Not me!" Christy said. "I'm putting on my jeans."

The others did the same, quickly dressing in a haphazard fashion.

"Let me get the key and some quarters," Christy said.

"Wait a minute!" Janelle ran into the bathroom. She emerged with the shower cap on her head and a bath towel wrapped around the outside of her clothes. "Now I'm ready!"

Brittany and Christy burst into laughter. It felt good to have the earlier tension with Brittany gone. Janelle opened the door and held her hand over her eyebrows, like a trail scout looking up and down the hallway.

"Okay, fellow adventurers," she said in a deep voice. "The coast is clear."

Repressing their giggles, the three girls clumped together and toddled down the hallway. They made it to the vending machines before anyone saw them and quickly pooled their quarters. They had enough for a candy bar each and one soft drink, which they decided they would split back in the room.

The vending machine made a loud rumbling noise as it

dropped out the can of soda. Janelle pressed her index finger to her lips, saying, "Shhhhh!" to the machine.

The other two giggled as they huddled together, and in unison all three looked down the hallway.

"What are we hiding from?" Christy asked.

"Shhhh!" Janelle motioned again. Then with exaggerated tip-toeing, Janelle led the way back to their room. Suddenly, they heard voices behind them and turned to see a young couple who had just gotten off the elevator and were heading in their direction.

"Hurry!" Janelle ordered, breaking into a dash for their room.

They were almost to Bob and Marti's door when Janelle let out a "Yikes!"

Christy ran to their door. She jammed in the key, turned the handle, and ducked inside as the other two pushed their way in behind her. Quickly, she slammed the door, and they all started laughing.

Christy pointed to Janelle. "What happened to your towel?"

"I lost it in front of your aunt and uncle's door! That's why I panicked."

"We've got to go get it," Christy said. "We can't leave it there!"

For almost a full minute, they squabbled over who would re-trieve the towel. Finally, Brittany settled the argument by stating, "All right, you cream puffs. I'll go get the towel."

Slowly, they opened the door and looked to the right, to the left, then they looked down at their feet. Someone had already picked up the towel, folded it neatly, and placed it in front of their door.

"One thing I can say about this hotel," Janelle said, snatching up the towel and quickly closing the door. "The maid service here is incredible!"

CHAPTER TEN

Making Choices

The next morning Brittany was the first one up, and she was brimming with energy.

"Wake up, you sleepyheads," she called. "Anyone interested in a morning jog?"

Janelle threw her pillow at Brittany. "Go away! It can't be morning yet."

"It's almost 8:30," Brittany sang out. "The day is slipping away while you two sleep."

"Wake me when it's noon," Christy said, pulling the covers over her head.

"I'll wake you deadheads when I get back."

Christy grunted and drifted back to sleep. She woke up with a start when the phone rang a short time later. It was Aunt Marti telling them to meet her for breakfast in half an hour at the Sundance Coffee Shop in the lobby.

Brittany returned from her morning jog, perspiring and breathless, and the three of them scrambled to get ready in time.

"I didn't know you were really going jogging," Christy said. "I don't think you should've gone out like that."

"Oh, I just went around the hotel. I was perfectly safe," Brittany said, applying her mascara with a shaky hand.

"Come on, you guys," Janelle hollered from the door. "Your aunt is probably waiting."

"What? No shower cap this morning?" Christy teased as she slipped past Janelle. The three of them hurried to catch the elevator.

Aunt Marti stood waiting in the entrance of the coffee shop. Right next to her stood the young couple from the night before. The three girls suppressed their giggles and kept their heads down.

As soon as they were seated, Aunt Marti laid out their plans for the day. They would spend some time by the pool relaxing and then go shopping; dinner would be at 6:30 at Bob's favorite Mexican restaurant.

"This is the way to live!" Janelle exclaimed to Christy a short time later. The poolside waitress was serving them iced teas they had ordered from their lounge chairs. "I've never been to a resort like this in my life. I just decided I could very easily be a rich person. It suits me, don't you think?"

Brittany was in the pool with her arms propped up on the side. She playfully flung a handful of water on them. "Hey you rich and famous wannabes, are you coming in or not?" Brittany yelled.

"I'm ready," Christy said. "Coming, Janelle?"

Janelle stretched like a spoiled cat and in her best movie-star voice said, "Oh, I suppose, darling. If I must."

The two girls slowly lowered themselves into the pool at the shallow end. Christy hated that shivering sensation that sliced through her every time she got her stomach wet. She quickly ducked the rest of her body underwater and swam leisurely, with Janelle dog-paddling beside her. Brittany kept challenging them to swim laps with her, as if it would be fun to start some kind of competitive race. Christy turned down all the offers, saying she was happy going at her own, slow pace.

Marti came out to the pool and settled in a lounge chair shaded by an umbrella. She waved at the girls and then motioned for the poolside attendant to come take her order for something to drink. Christy thought her aunt looked as if she were enjoying this as much as they were. She knew Marti would also enjoy the planned shopping trip that afternoon. What Christy was really looking forward to was the promised hot air balloon ride. Maybe tomorrow.

Brittany pulled herself out of the pool at the deep end after swimming several laps by herself. "I think your aunt's trying to tell us she's ready to go shopping," Brittany said. "Mind if I go in first and take a quick shower?"

"Go ahead. We'll be there in a few minutes," Christy said. "The key is in my bag under my chair."

Christy and Janelle got out of the pool and patted themselves dry with the thick hotel beach towels.

"Were you trying to tell us it's time to go shopping?" Christy asked Aunt Marti.

Aunt Marti, who sat only a few feet away, ignored Christy's question and seemed to be studying Brittany's skeletonlike frame as she walked away from them.

"I think your friend is far too thin," Marti said. "I've never seen hip bones stick out like that on a teenager. It doesn't look right. And where's her rear end? She hardly has enough bottom to hold her bathing suit on."

Christy didn't know how much she wanted to confide in her aunt, but Janelle jumped right in. "We know. She's got some strange problems with food. She's always on a diet and then she overeats and makes herself throw up."

"I've read about girls like her," Marti said in her direct manner. "She needs professional help to overcome this problem.

Eating disorders are very common and also very dangerous. Thank goodness that's something Christy hasn't struggled with! You've always had a healthy appetite, dear."

Christy couldn't tell if her comment was a put-down or a compliment.

"Well," Janelle said, "I'd feel awful if anything bad happened to her. Like if she got really sick or something. What should we do?"

"Leave it to me. I'll handle this," Marti stated.

For some reason, Christy felt a knot forming in her stomach at her aunt's words. Marti was a well-meaning woman, but she had messed up things for Christy more than once. How would she handle Brittany?

About an hour later, after quick showers and an even quicker scramble to dress, Marti steered them through the streets of Palm Springs as if she were in her hometown. She took the girls to several small boutiques where they received plenty of personal attention.

Marti talked Christy into getting a short, black dress that Brittany said she had seen in one of her fashion magazines that month. Janelle said it made Christy look at least 17.

Oh, great! Christy thought as she surveyed herself in the mirror. *The last thing I need is another dress that makes me look older! What will Dad say?*

But Marti insisted, and in the end, they left the boutique with the dress, some fun, strappy black shoes to match, and a pair of dangly earrings that Christy thought were way too expensive, even if they were a custom design.

Christy and Janelle slid into the backseat of the car, and Janelle said softly, "Now you have something to wear to Homecoming when we go on our double date with Rick and Greg. I figured out a way to get the guys to go with us. I'll tell you about it later."

Christy forced a weak smile. *Homecoming? Double dates? Who said I even wanted to go out with Rick? When am I going to start standing up for what I truly think and feel and stop letting everybody else make decisions for me? Like this dress. I don't even like it. Why did I let my aunt buy it?*

The next place they went was the Desert Fashion Plaza. The minute they entered Saks, Christy knew they were about to see some serious money being spent. Marti reminded her of a tropical bird that had suddenly been transported to its native banana tree. Watching Marti coo and strut between the racks of clothes, Christy could just picture her aunt pulling out her credit cards and fanning them like a peacock's tail.

This time I'm going to decide for myself, Christy vowed.

All three of the girls entered the large, elegant dressing area. The saleswoman had already hung their choices on the outside of three individual rooms, and now she stood ready to serve them in any way she could.

Christy was the first to call out from her dressing room. "I think this shirt is a little too big on me."

"What size is it?" the saleswoman asked. "I'll bring you another one."

"Step out, dear. Let's see the whole outfit." Aunt Marti smiled when she saw Christy. "Oh, yes, I like those bright colors on you very much. Very striking."

Christy looked in the full-length mirror. Several months earlier she would have eaten up every word her aunt said, along with all the glamour and excitement that accompanied such a trip as this. But this time she forced herself to see the outfit clearly, from her own point of view. She didn't like it. Time to practice standing up for herself. *No, no, no, no.*

"I don't know," she said cautiously to her aunt. "I'm not a bold, striking type of person. I think I like the peach better."

"Let's see," Janelle said, stepping out in a long rayon dress. She made a face at Christy that only confirmed Christy's opinion of how she looked in this outfit. "I think I need a bigger size on this dress," Janelle said to the saleswoman. "It's too tight under the arms."

The saleswoman checked the tag and then left. Marti paused a minute, tapping her index finger along the side of her mouth. "I suppose you're right, Christy. You wear peach very nicely, especially that deep salmon shade."

Christy held up a light peach shirt. "This is the peach I mean. Light peach. Pastel. What do you think?"

Marti blinked her eyes, as if her feelings were hurt, but then her expression softened, and with a chuckle, she said, "I think it obviously doesn't matter what I think. You've made up your own mind. And that's very commendable, Christina. Did you match it with your color swatches?"

Christy ducked back into the dressing room and rummaged through all the junk in her purse, trying to find her color packet. The packet came from a color consultant Marti took Christy to last summer. The consultant had evaluated Christy's natural coloring and provided her with a collection of color swatches.

The consultant had instructed Christy to never wear a color that wasn't in her packet. Now if only she could find the packet in her messy purse!

Her hand circled around a small plastic prescription bottle, and she suddenly froze. *Brittany's diet pills! I have to get rid of these! But not here. Not in front of Marti, especially now that she's noticed that Brittany has a problem. She'll think I'm trying out Brittany's crazy diet techniques. As soon as we get back to the hotel, I'm getting rid of these. And I'm not giving them back to Brittany. I'm going to throw them away.*

"Absolutely adorable," Christy overheard her aunt say to her friends outside the dressing room. The color swatches forgotten,

Christy hurried to take off the outfit. She was eager to get back to the hotel.

"Now, listen," Marti said to Janelle and Brittany. "I'd like to buy each of you one new outfit, so choose whatever you like. It'll be my treat."

"Really?" Janelle squeaked. "That's so nice of you! I can't believe it."

"You don't have to," Brittany said. "My dad gave me his Visa card in case I wanted to buy anything."

"Well, let me buy it for you, dear. I'd like to do that. Do you like the outfit you have on?"

"Pretty much," Brittany answered. "I was thinking of getting it."

"That settles it; I'll get it for you," Marti offered. "It looks nice on you, although the shorts are a bit baggy in the back, don't you think?"

Oh no! Christy squeezed her eyes shut in the privacy of her dressing room. *Here comes my aunt's subtle way of dealing with Brittany's weight problem.*

"It's the smallest size they have," Brittany answered. "I like them baggy. They make me look thinner."

"Honey, you are about as thin as a person can possibly get. How much do you weigh, dear?"

Brittany didn't answer right away. "I don't know. I haven't weighed myself lately."

"In my opinion, dear, you could stand to put on a few pounds. Start eating some good, healthy pasta and bread at every meal."

Christy slowly opened the door to see Brittany's reaction to Marti's words. Marti had turned abruptly away from Brittany and was evaluating Janelle's outfit. "Now with your dark hair, dear, you shouldn't wear such a deep shade right next to your face. What about that mint green sweater I suggested? Ah, here it is. Janelle, this would be a gorgeous shade on you, don't you think?"

The rest of the afternoon and the evening continued the same way, with Marti in control. When they got back to the hotel, Marti stayed in their room directing each of them on what to wear to dinner. Marti insisted that Christy wear her new black dress. Even though the other girls and Bob made all kinds of flattering comments during the night, Christy still didn't feel like herself. She felt Marti was trying to make her into someone else, and she didn't know how that "someone else" should sit or speak or smile.

Bob was acquainted with the owners of the Mexican restaurant they went to and asked the waiter if "Joaquin" was running the show that night.

Soon a tall, handsome, dark-haired man appeared at the table, and Bob rose to greet him with a hearty handshake. "How've you been, Roberto?" the man asked. "And Marti, you become more beautiful every time I see you!"

Marti held out her hand, and Joaquin kissed it, then raised his head to view the three girls. "And who do we have here? You have been holding out on me, Roberto!"

"Joaquin, I'd like you to meet my one and only niece, Christina, and her friends, Janelle and Brittany."

Joaquin shook Brittany's hand, "Beautiful hair," he said. "Like the golden sunshine on the desert sand."

As he shook Janelle's hand, he said, "Your smile could light the darkest night."

Then turning to Christy, he smiled and said, "Christina, Christina." The "r's" rolled off his tongue with great flair. "You have eyes like rare gems. Never have I seen eyes like yours. One look into those eyes, and a man is taken captive forever."

Christy turned away, feeling herself blush from her neck up.

"Such innocence," Joaquin said to Bob. "It is beautiful on a woman."

Changing his tone and addressing everyone at the table, he said, "Listen, my friends, tonight you must try the crab enchiladas. They are the best."

"That sound good to everybody?" Bob asked.

"I'll just have half of a chicken tostada with the guacamole on the side," Marti said. Then she added, "Brittany, you be sure to order enough, dear. Order anything you like."

All three girls and Bob ordered the crab enchiladas. Christy thought they were delicious. They were mild, for Mexican food, and covered with cheese. She knew it must be the influence of growing up on a Wisconsin dairy farm, but that was just the way she liked her Mexican food. After eating her entire dinner, Christy felt so full she didn't think she could stand up.

The waiter came to clear their plates and said, "Your dinner is on the house tonight, sir. Would you care for anything else?"

"Girls?" Bob asked.

"I couldn't eat another bite!" Janelle said.

The others agreed.

"I guess that's it," Bob said. "Tell Joaquin thanks for us. The crab enchiladas were terrific. And here, this is for you." Bob handed the waiter a $50 bill.

"Thank you, sir!" the waiter said, his eyes wide with surprise. "Thank you very much!"

"Robert," Marti scolded in a low voice, "don't you think you overtipped him a bit?"

"That's the smallest I had. Besides, the dinner was free." He turned to Christy and her wide-eyed friends. "So how about it, girls. You ready for a movie?"

"As long as you don't buy us any popcorn," Janelle said. "I'm so full."

"How about you, Brittany?" Marti asked pointedly. "Did you get enough to eat?"

"Yes, I did. Thank you." Christy thought Brittany sounded like a robot answering Marti's obvious questions. She wondered if she sounded that cold and rude when she answered her aunt during the times when Marti bugged her.

"Then let's go, shall we, Robert?"

When they arrived at the theater, they found the film was sold out, and the next showing was at 10:10. After much debate, they finally agreed to go back to the hotel and go to bed. They would all meet in the lobby for brunch in the morning, if any of them felt like eating by then.

The girls lounged in their room, watching TV and feeling bloated and lazy.

Brittany went into the bathroom, and Janelle jumped up to turn down the TV.

"Listen," she whispered to Christy. "She's doing it again. She's throwing up."

"I can't say at this moment that I don't feel like throwing up myself," Christy said.

"I know, but she did it this afternoon, too. When we came back from the pool. She didn't think I heard her, but I did."

"She told me she wasn't doing that anymore," Christy said.

"She told you a lot of other things, too," Janelle said, looking very serious. "This isn't good. I think we should try to help her. After all the things your aunt said at the pool, I'm really worried."

"I know, but what can we do?" Christy said softly.

"We could try talking to her about it," Janelle suggested.

Right then, the bathroom door opened, and Brittany came back into the room. She realized the two girls had taken their eyes off the TV and were focusing on her. Janelle turned off the TV and looked over at Christy and then back at Brittany.

"What?" Brittany said. "What's wrong?"

Christy didn't know what to say. Janelle was the gutsy one. Christy hoped Janelle would start this difficult conversation.

"Brit, well, it's like this," Janelle said. "We know you've been trying to lose weight and everything, and you've lost a lot of weight already. Really fast, too."

Brittany stood perfectly still. Her face was expressionless.

"And, well, we're worried because it's not good for you to throw up a lot, and we know that you have been."

Brittany's face softened. "I know. I don't want to throw up. I'm not trying to. It's just that I've had this terrible stomachache all day. I didn't want to tell anyone because I didn't want to ruin the shopping trip and everything for the rest of you. I think my stomach just couldn't handle those heavy enchiladas tonight."

"Why didn't you say something?" Christy asked. "Are you feeling better now?"

"Not really. My stomach is still upset."

"Can we do anything to help you?" Janelle asked, her face showing her sincere concern. "Do you want Christy to check with her uncle and see if he has anything you could take for your upset stomach?"

"No," Brittany said, sitting on the edge of the bed. She folded her arms across her middle and let out a little groan. "I think I'll just go to the drugstore and get some antacid tablets. I know that would help. When I was out jogging this morning, I went past a drugstore about a block from here."

"I'll get my uncle to take you," Christy said, reaching for the phone. "What's their room number?"

"No! Please!" Brittany insisted. "I don't want to bother them. They're probably already asleep, and after all the things your aunt was saying to me today, the last thing I want to do is get on her bad side. I'll run to the drugstore by myself."

"You can't go by yourself," Janelle protested.

"I did this morning."

"That was different. It was daylight then. Muggers and weirdos don't work when the sun's up," Janelle said. "We'll go with you."

"I don't think we should," Christy said.

"It's only a block away," Brittany said. "Maybe less."

"We left our room last night, and nobody knew it," Janelle reasoned. "I think Brittany's right. We shouldn't bother your aunt and uncle for something minor like a little roll of antacids."

"I don't know, you guys," Christy said. "I don't feel right about it."

"Look, Christy," Janelle said, pulling her thick, wavy, black hair back in a scrunchie. "The weekend is only half over. The last thing we want to do is get your aunt upset at us for waking her up and disrupting her beauty sleep. Besides, if you were the one with the upset stomach, Brittany would go to the drugstore with you. Wouldn't you, Brit?"

"Oh, definitely. We'll only be gone for five minutes. They'll never know. You don't have to come with us, Christy."

Christy absolutely hated moments like this! She had never been good at making split-second decisions. She hated the feeling of being an outcast, yet she knew they shouldn't leave the hotel by themselves at night.

"Listen," Janelle said quietly to Christy while Brittany looked in the closet for some shoes. "This is a way we could really help Brittany. You're the one who said we should try to be her friend and help her."

"I know, but . . ."

"Come on. It'll be fun. The drugstore is right next door. Isn't that what she said? It might even be part of the hotel."

"She said it was a block away."

"Okay, a block. Christy, we should think of Brittany now, not ourselves." Janelle slipped on her sandals and went over to the door next to Brittany.

"We're going," Janelle said. "Now are you coming with us or not?"

"Oh, all right." Christy spit the words out and jumped up from the bed. "Where's my purse? I don't want to get locked out. You sure it's only a block away?"

"Maybe a block and a half. It's not far. Trust me," Brittany said, opening the door.

Janelle imitated their antics of the night before, looking up and down the hallway before exiting. "Come on," Janelle whispered to Christy. "The coast is clear!"

Reluctantly, Christy stepped into the hallway. The door automatically locked behind them.

CHAPTER ELEVEN

Midnight Run

"How much farther is it, Brittany? We've already gone over two blocks!" Christy felt as panicked as she sounded.

"It's down this street, here," Brittany said calmly. "You surprise me, Christy. After we papered Rick's house, I thought you were a professional at late-night adventures on dark streets."

Christy clenched her teeth. *Am I being a baby?* She shot a glance at Janelle.

Janelle's usual carefree look had disappeared. Anger now spread across her face. "I think it's too far," Janelle said. "Let's go back and ask Christy's uncle to drive us."

"Hey, if you guys want to go back, that's fine with me," Brittany said. "But I'm going to the drugstore. Look. There it is." Brittany stepped up her pace, and the other two trotted along beside her.

Inside the brightly lit store, Christy felt a little more secure. The trip actually seemed rational once they could see other people, normal people, standing in the checkout lines, buying normal things. Still, her heart pounded with the fear that if her parents ever knew she did this, she would be in big trouble.

Why didn't I chicken out? she thought. *I wish I'd stayed back at the hotel. Why am I doing this?*

"Over here," Janelle called from one of the well-stocked aisles. "What kind of antacid do you want? Hurry, so we can go back."

"I don't know. You look at what they have. I'll be right back." Brittany shot like an arrow to the back of the store.

"Where's she going?" Christy asked.

"I don't know, but we'd better find out."

Janelle and Christy found Brittany at the pharmacy window, reaching for a small bag the clerk held out to her.

"What's she doing?" Janelle asked.

"Oh, no!" Christy felt a rush of horror through her veins. "I hope that's not what I think it is."

"What?"

Christy stepped up to Brittany as she turned to walk away from the counter and boldly confronted her, "Are those your mom's diet pills?"

"What do you mean?" Brittany returned a blank stare.

"Brittany!" Janelle reprimanded. "You don't even have a mother! What are you trying to do?"

The window to the pharmacy area was still open, and the clerk stood there, casually observing the girls.

"Janelle, it's not funny when you act like this. I don't appreciate it at all. You know my mom asked me to pick up her medicine for her." Brittany's eyes opened wide as she coaxed Janelle to go along with the story. "Come on. We're going to be late, and she'll be really mad."

Janelle looked as if she might explode with anger at any moment. "Come on, Christy," she said, turning and pulling Christy by the arm. "You and I are leaving. I can't believe she did this to us!"

"I just figured it out," Christy said as they marched down the hair-care aisle. "Brittany must have left the empty prescription bottle here this morning when she said she went jogging. This whole scene tonight with the stomachache was to get us to go with her to pick up her diet pills.''

"Right. And we were dumb enough to fall for it. We're going back to the hotel—now.''

"I can't believe she lied to us. I can't believe I didn't just tell her no!'' Christy moaned.

"We don't have to tell anybody,'' Janelle said over her shoulder as they neared the front of the store. "Let's hurry back to our room and wait for Brittany. If she gets caught, we'll say she snuck out without us.''

"Janelle, we can't lie!''

"Why not? She lied to us! Do you think we should wait here and help her pay for her pills or something?''

Just then Brittany rounded the end of the next aisle and met them at the front of the store. She looked as if she'd run to get ahead of them, but other than that, seemed unaffected by the whole scene. "You guys ready to go?''

Christy and Janelle exchanged looks of confusion. "Aren't you going to buy something?'' Christy asked.

"No,'' Brittany answered calmly. She stepped toward the exit and the glass doors opened automatically for her.

Christy felt completely flustered and confused. All she wanted to do was get back to the hotel so this whole night could be over.

Suddenly, a voice boomed behind them. "Ladies, hold up a minute there.''

A large man dressed in a security guard uniform towered over them. "Would you young ladies come with me?'' his voice demanded.

Numbed and silent, they followed him back into the store to a small office. Brittany hung behind at first, then all of a sudden she tugged at Christy's purse and hung onto the strap. Christy could feel the purse strap dig into her shoulder as Brittany whispered, "We don't have to take this, you know. We have rights. Remember what Ms. Archer is always telling us?"

"Forget it, Brittany. This is the last time I let you talk me into anything, and I mean it!"

The guard pushed open the door to a small office. It felt unbearably hot inside the small room.

"Have a seat," he commanded, pointing to a narrow couch in the corner. They squished next to each other while the guard swung open the back door to let in the evening air.

"Stupid air conditioner," he mumbled. "I need to ask you girls a few questions." Turning his back on them, he adjusted the thermostat on the air conditioner.

"Come on!" Brittany hissed. She grabbed Janelle's arm, and the two of them vanished out the open door.

Christy jumped up, then sat down, then jumped up again.

"Sit down," the guard bellowed.

Instantly, she obeyed.

"Stay where you are!" the guard ordered and dashed out into the darkness.

Christy trembled. Everything within her fought the urge to run. *It's just like the night we papered Rick's house! They ran off and left me again. What am I going to do? What's going to happen?* Christy drew in a deep breath, her chest pounding. *I can't believe this is happening! What am I going to do?*

In the stillness, a sudden thought pierced her. Something she had read: "Do not be afraid."

It was part of the verse in Tracy's letter! Christy grabbed the envelope from the side pocket of her purse and pulled out the card.

She read it slowly, " 'The Lord himself goes before you and will be with you; he will never leave you nor forsake you. Do not be afraid; do not be discouraged.' "

Christy felt a quietness trickling over her like a warm shower. She read the verse again and again. The comforting sensation continued to calm her. It was as if Jesus were sitting right beside her, putting His arm around her, talking softly to her. She never heard a voice or anything. But it was the closest she had felt to the Lord since last summer.

Suddenly, the guard appeared in the doorway, perspiring and heaving deep breaths. "Your friends must be experienced at running away." He pulled out a handkerchief, wiped his forehead, and then positioned himself on the edge of the desk.

"Don't make this any harder on yourself. First of all," he began, "how old are you?"

"Fifteen." Then she added, "Sir."

He pulled out a notebook and began writing. "Okay, that's one. Violation of curfew. Not something you want to mess with in Palm Springs. What's your name?"

"Christy Miller, or, well, Christina Miller, sir."

"Your parents' name and address?"

She rattled off her address and then went into a jumbled explanation of how she was in Palm Springs with her aunt and uncle.

"Where are you staying? What hotel?"

"Um, I think it's the West something . . . I don't remember. Oh, maybe it's on my room key." With sweaty hands, Christy pulled her purse up to her lap and reached for the key.

Suddenly, she froze. The first thing her hand touched was a crackly paper bag—a slick, white pharmacy bag.

"May I see that?" the guard asked, reaching for the bag that Brittany had so slyly slipped into Christy's purse.

"It's not mine," Christy said defensively. "I didn't take it."

"Where's the receipt for these?" he asked, pulling out three boxes of laxatives.

Christy gasped. "I-I don't know. They're not mine!"

"You're saying these aren't yours either?" He held up the prescription diet pills.

"No! No! They're not mine! Really!"

"We'll let the police decide about that." He continued to go through her purse, dumping the contents on the table. He flipped through her wallet, fanned through her color swatches, and then lifted up a prescription bottle, held it to his ear, and shook it. Two pills rattled inside.

Oh no! No! Christy screamed under her breath. *No! No! Why didn't I throw those stupid pills out the day Brittany gave them to me? I can't believe they're still in there!*

The guard read the prescription, then opened the bottle and examined the tiny pills in the palm of his hand. Christy's eyes burned with tears as he opened the new prescription bottle of the same diet pills and compared them.

"I suppose these aren't yours either?"

"No, sir. They were given to me. They've been there for weeks." The words jerked their way out of her throat in spasms.

"I see," he said, writing furiously in his notebook. Then he picked up the phone and talked to somebody named Pat.

"Yeah, Pat," he said. "I've got a curfew violation with a possible illegal possession. Tourist. Sure. I'll have the report finished by the time you get here." He hung up the phone and continued writing.

"Can I go now?" Christy asked meekly.

"Can you go? I don't think so, missy. You're caught, young lady. The jig is up, as they say. Your whole life is about to change. You sit tight. The police are on their way."

Police! Why? I told the truth. They're not my pills. Christy couldn't sit still. Her body throbbed with the drumming of her heart. She felt the perspiration rolling down the front of her, soaking her shirt, forming a river around her waist. Her mind pulsated as each terrifying thought rode on a different vein, shooting wildly through her head. *Why is this happening to me? Where did Brittany and Janelle go? Why did they leave me?*

The door of the office opened and in stepped a short, thickset police officer with a wide, bushy mustache. "Yeesh! Sure is hot in here. Air conditioner broken again?"

"Yeah, Pat. How you doing?"

"All right. Is this the suspect?"

"Right. Her name is Miller, Cathy."

"Christy," she corrected him. Her voice came out squeaky like a screen door closing.

They both ignored her. The security guard handed the police officer the report forms he had been filling out. "There are two others. Females, same age roughly. They bolted. This one had enough sense to face the music."

"I see. Cathy, what are your friends' names?"

"Christy." She still sounded squeaky.

"One of them is Christy? And the other?" The officer pulled out a pen and began writing on the report forms.

"No, see, my name is Christy. Christy Miller. Or, well, Christina Miller. You called me Cathy."

"I see. Okay, Christy. What are the names of the other two girls?"

"Janelle Layne and Brittany Taylor. They live in Escondido."

"And who is Merriah Jasmine Taylor?"

"I don't know."

"Are you sure?" The officer held up the diet pill bottle to read the name on the label again.

"Oh, that must be Brittany's mom. I've never met her. They're divorced. Her parents, I mean. Brittany's parents. She lives with her dad. His name is Hank Taylor."

"Okay, okay." The officer stopped her. "That's fine. Let's go down to the station and finish this. These charges are rather serious. Did you know that?"

Christy shook her head and looked at him blankly.

"Miss Miller, you have the right to remain silent. Should you give up that right, anything you say can and will be used against you in a court of law...." The officer continued reciting her rights as if she were a crook or something. It all seemed like a bad scene from some TV rerun.

"Come with me," the officer said. He took her arm and held it all the way to the police car. People in the parking lot were looking at her. She bent down and slid into the backseat. Straight ahead of her, the grille between the front seat and the back made her feel caged in and helpless. They drove the mile or so to the Palm Springs Police Station with only the crackling messages on the police radio breaking the dead silence of the night.

Christy trembled all over. Her lower jaw shivered until her teeth chattered. She kept trying to repeat the verse over and over again, " 'The Lord himself goes before you and will be with you; he will never leave you nor forsake you. Do not be afraid; do not be discouraged.' " Every time she said it, she felt a little stronger, a little more clear-headed.

They entered the police station lobby. The officer went up to the front desk, and Christy tried to ignore the other people around her and keep her knees from shaking so much. She focused her attention on a picture on the wall. It was a print she had seen before of a small boy and a large police officer sitting beside each other on counter stools at a diner. The boy looked as though he had tried to run away from home, but the officer had found him and was treating him to a little snack. Christy never thought she would be living out the part of the runaway. And her officer didn't look as if he were about to treat her to anything.

"Follow me," he said, leading her down a hall to a small room with a table and three chairs. "Have a seat. Now tell me about the laxatives and pills found in your possession. Where did you get them?"

"My friend Brittany stuck them in my purse. They were hers."

"But the prescription was made out to Merriah Taylor, not Brittany Taylor."

"I guess, I mean, they were originally her mom's, or at least the prescription was her mom's, but Brittany got them refilled today and picked them up tonight. That's why we were out after curfew. But we really thought she was sick. Janelle and I. Brittany was sick, I mean. We didn't know she was just using us."

"Let's start over," the officer said.

Christy slowed down and carefully told him the whole situation, starting back with how they came to Palm Springs with her aunt and uncle. She explained how Brittany had given her the diet pills found in her purse weeks ago, and she had only carried them around but never took them.

"Do you realize that you were in possession of illegal drugs that whole time?"

Christy shook her head. "No, sir. She told me they were just diet pills."

"Prescription diet pills. Prescribed for someone else, not for you. That's nothing to mess with. It's a health and safety code violation. Drug-related violation. This will go on your record."

"But, but, I—"

"I want you to know I believe you're telling the truth about holding the drugs for your friend and that you never took any. However, you were in possession of the shoplifted items and prescription drugs, obtained through falsification. We'll have to hold you until we can contact your aunt and uncle."

Christy sat perfectly still, yet her mind jumped and twisted and hopped at a frenzied pace. She thought of the illustration in Sunday school when Peter Pagan so easily yanked Katie Christian down to his level.

It can happen so fast! What if I'd taken the laxatives and diet pills like Brittany wanted me to? If only I'd said no tonight. If only I'd stayed at the hotel room—none of this would have happened.

Then Christy remembered Leslie saying that you could go crazy trying to live in the Land of If Only. *I've got to believe God is in control, even now.*

An officer took Christy to be "printed." Each finger was rolled in black ink. As she stood there, looking at her 10 blackened fingertips, she felt dirty.

What was that verse from Sunday school? Something about "bad company corrupting good character"? Christy felt corrupted as she tried to wipe the black ink off her fingers with a rough paper towel.

A woman officer, the keys jingling on her belt, led Christy down a hall past a row of cells. They stopped in a small room with a camera. Christy was directed to stand on a mark on the floor while a mechanical arm moved in front of her. She trembled all over when she realized that the mechanical arm displayed a number. A jailbird number, black and white.

She looked forward, and the camera snapped with a blinding flash. She turned to face the wall, and a second picture was taken. Never, ever in her life had Christy felt like this—so utterly humiliated and completely misunderstood. She felt dirty and ugly and bad. And to make it worse, this whole painful experience was being recorded. Kept on file. Captured with a picture.

"The suspect's guardians have arrived," an officer said, poking his head in the room a short time later. "I'll take her."

Christy was led back to the lobby, where Bob, Marti, and

Janelle sat on a bench. She approached them cautiously, her head down. Then she spotted Brittany standing to the side, holding her head high, looking cool, calm, and confident.

"Christina Juliet Miller!" Aunt Marti sprang from her seat. "I hope you realize what kind of trouble you're in! Running out in the middle of the—"

"I'll handle this, Martha." Bob reached over and squeezed Christy's shoulder. "You all right?"

She nodded, her eyes filling with tears. "I'm sorry, Uncle Bob. We shouldn't have left our room. I'm so, so sorry."

"Okay." The police officer named Pat stood before them with a bunch of papers in his hand. "I'm sure you folks are anxious to get this cleared up. Let me take the girls one at a time. Janelle, I'd like to talk to you first."

Janelle's usual carefree, just-flew-in-from-Tahiti look had disappeared. She looked as shaken up as Christy felt. With cautious steps, Janelle followed the officer down the hall.

Brittany appeared completely unaffected. She stood, rather than sat, and looked out the front door into the darkness, as if she were involved in something going on outside.

How can you be so detached from this, Brittany? Christy thought. *I feel sorry for you.*

Christy realized that as much as she'd wanted to be Brittany's friend and help her, there was something much more complicated going on here. Maybe Brittany needed more than a friend right now. Maybe she needed to get "caught."

"Did you tell the officer the truth, Christina?" Aunt Marti asked, grabbing Christy's arm and digging her fingernails into the flesh.

"Ouch!"

Marti released her grip. "Tell me, dear. What happened?"

"I told him everything I knew. I told the truth."

Brittany snapped her focus onto Christy and pierced her with the most spiteful look Christy had ever received.

"Of course she told the truth!" Bob defended. "I'd never expect anything but the truth from this young woman. She's a woman of honor." His look, his words, his warm arm around her shoulder, drenched Christy with a healing she desperately needed. It left her weak. It brought release.

As if all the plugs had been suddenly pulled from her pent-up emotions, Christy doubled over, dropped her head in her hands, and wept a thousand salty tears.

"Whatever is the matter with her, Robert?" Marti snipped. "What did you say to the poor child?"

"Let her cry, Martha. Just let her cry."

As Christy tried to curtail her tears, her aunt rose and walked calmly over to Brittany.

"Brittany," Marti began sweetly, "is there anything you'd like to talk about before the officer questions you?"

Christy pulled up her head and dried her eyes, listening intently for Brittany's response.

"No."

"Now, dear, I'm sure you realize this is all very important, and we are here to help you in any way we can."

Brittany pulled away. Aunt Marti didn't. She was used to having her way. Her voice raised, her head tall, her face directly pointed toward Brittany, she said, "Do you realize we have a serious problem here? You need professional help, child."

Brittany slowly coiled back, like a snake about to strike. Then she thrust her head and her voice forward with a loud burst of laughter.

Stunned, Marti turned to Bob for support. None of them knew what to do or what to expect next. Brittany kept laughing until the tears rolled down her cheeks, and Marti stood in utter silence. Then the officer returned with Janelle and asked to see Brittany.

Wiping the tears and still chuckling to herself, Brittany followed Officer Pat.

"What's with her?" Janelle asked.

"I don't know," Christy answered, wiping her eyes with a tissue Marti handed her. "What happened with you?"

"He asked me a bunch of stuff, and I told him what I knew. He said he believed me, and that was all."

"What happened after you guys ran out of the drugstore?"

Janelle positioned herself sideways next to Christy on the wooden bench and looked up at the picture of the little boy and the policeman above them. "I always liked that picture. My dad has a big book of pictures by that artist."

Bob twisted his neck to see. "Norman Rockwell," he said. "My all-time favorite."

"Janelle!" Christy squawked. "Forget about the picture, and tell me what happened!"

"First Brittany grabbed my arm and pulled me out of that little office. I guess I could have broken away from her, but I didn't know what to do. We hid behind a big Dumpster at the back of the store and waited until the security guard went back inside."

"Why did you do that?"

"I don't know. Why did we do any of it? It all happened so fast. I wanted to go back to the hotel, but I said we didn't have the key, and then Brittany said, 'Oh, don't we?' She held up the room key and said you gave it to her."

"I did not! She took it out of my purse and left me with the bag from the pharmacy."

"You're kidding!"

"No, I'm not kidding! That's why I got in so much trouble. They thought I was the one getting the prescription drugs. Plus, there were three packages of laxatives in the bag, which she apparently didn't intend to pay for."

"You mean she was going to steal them?"

"I guess so. At least that's what the guard accused me of doing when he called the police."

Janelle leaned her head against the wall. "What a mess! Brittany said they'd let you go. You're a minor. I never thought they'd call the police."

"So, what did you guys do? Jog back to the hotel and think you'd wait around for me to come waltzing back? Thanks a lot."

"No, wait!" Janelle said. "Let me finish. We practically ran back to the hotel. Brittany didn't want me to, but I went right over to your aunt and uncle's room and woke them and told them everything."

"Then Janelle and I drove straight to the drugstore, but they said you'd been brought here," Bob said. "So we went back to the hotel, picked up Brittany and Marti, and came down here. Janelle told me everything, Christy. Don't accuse yourself too harshly. It's clear that the fault lies with Brittany. You made the mistake of not saying no when it really mattered."

"I wonder what's going to happen to her," Christy said.

"Perhaps you should wonder what's going to happen to you, Christina. This is no laughing matter," Marti scolded.

The officer stepped into the lobby without Brittany and addressed them. "Okay, the story checks out. The charges against your niece will be minimal. She'll have this on her record—possession, shoplifting suspect—but she can have her record sealed once she turns 18. Something like this shouldn't ruin a kid's whole life." He sounded softer, more human now and less like the bulldog he had seemed to be earlier.

"What about Brittany?" Christy asked.

"What about me?" Janelle asked.

"Okay, Janelle, you did the right thing in contacting the adults. Your only charge is curfew violation. Under the circumstances, we'll let that go."

"Are you going to have to call my parents tonight?" Janelle asked.

"We already have. They agreed that we could release you to your friend's aunt and uncle here. We're holding Brittany until we can reach her father. He doesn't seem to be home."

The thought of the police officer calling her parents made Christy feel sick. Bravely, she ventured the question, "Did you call my parents?"

"Yes, we did. I might add, they weren't too happy about the situation, miss. Actually"—the officer glanced at his watch—"it's almost midnight. Let me talk to the sergeant and see if we can't release Brittany to you tonight. She'll have to appear before a judge for sentencing in about a month."

"Will she come back here?" Bob asked.

"No. The Indio County Courthouse. She'll probably appear before a juvenile referee. My guess is that they'll require her to enroll in a treatment program for her eating disorder. They might place her on probation. Require her to do some kind of community service work."

"Will the program help her eating problems?" Christy asked. "I'm really worried about her."

The officer paused a moment and then answered in the most human-sounding voice he had used yet. "Let me tell you about kids with eating disorders. My brother's kid was 16 when they finally put her in a hospital program. She weighed only 82 pounds the day they admitted her. She was in there for months.

"Seemed to like it, being with a whole ward full of 'her kind' and having a shrink to talk to whenever she felt like it. My brother shelled out thousands of bucks to get her straightened out. She died. They found her on the bathroom floor in the hospital with a box of laxatives in her hand. Some friend had smuggled them in to her. She was a beautiful girl. Could have had a great future . . ." His voice trailed off.

Christy and Janelle looked at each other in stunned silence.

"I knew it was serious," Marti spoke up. "I tried to tell that girl, but she simply wouldn't listen. Let this be a lesson to the two of you!" She eyed Janelle and Christy.

"Girls like that need help," the officer said. "It's as though there's a voice in their heads telling them they're fat and they need to be thin because once they're thin, they can do anything, have anything, be anything."

He turned to Janelle and Christy and said, "I'm sure you two meant well, trying to help your friend tonight. Fact is, she needs more help than the two of you could give her. If you don't mind me giving you a bit of advice, I'd encourage you to think twice before you let somebody else lead you into foolish mischief. It could change your whole future."

CHAPTER TWELVE

One Quiet Word

The car stereo in the Mercedes played elevator music while Bob hummed along. Marti silently flipped through her magazine. The three girls sat perfectly still in the backseat. No one said a word.

Christy stared out the window at the dry desert scenery as they sped away from Palm Springs and headed home. The mid-morning light brushed the landscape with its amber hues. Already the heat rose from the pavement like iridescent snakes, charmed by the sun.

Right now, we should be riding in a hot air balloon or going up the aerial tramway or at least swimming in the hotel's pool. But now all the fun is over, and I have to face my parents. They are never going to understand. Christy felt miserable.

That morning they had packed in a rush and checked out of their hotel early. The night before, the police sergeant had agreed to release Brittany to Uncle Bob as long as she would be returned home to her father the next day.

Christy's mind played with nightmarish scenes of what her parents would say when she got home. She closed her eyes and prayed. She tried to remember the verse Tracy sent her and say it over and over. *The Lord Himself goes before you . . .*

Around 11:00, Bob pulled up in front of Christy's house. She bravely got out of the car, walked up the front steps, and opened the door. Her parents, Janelle's mom, and Mr. Taylor were all sitting at the kitchen table.

"Where's Brittany?" Mr. Taylor said, jumping up.

"In the car," Christy answered, checking her parents' faces for an indication of how they would deal with her. She felt weak and empty and wanted to run to them and feel their reassuring hugs. At the same time she wanted to stand her ground and tell them she wasn't a baby anymore. She'd grown up, and they could trust her now more than ever because she was determined not to meekly follow others.

Mr. Taylor hurried out the front door. Christy watched as he greeted Bob and spoke with him briefly. Brittany emerged from the car with Janelle right behind her. Mr. Taylor hustled his daughter into his BMW. He seemed nervous and embarrassed when he called out, "Thanks again, Bob. See you folks later."

Bob pulled the suitcases from the car. It was uncomfortably quiet. Christy, her parents, and Janelle's mom had all joined the group outside. Janelle's mom reached for Janelle's luggage, but Christy's dad offered to carry it to the car for her.

"I guess we kind of messed up the weekend," Janelle said, giving Bob an apologetic look.

Janelle's mom sliced through the tension with a laugh. "Good heavens! I did worse things than sneaking out of a hotel room when I was a teenager. What matters most is that no one was hurt. I'm thankful for that."

Janelle and Christy exchanged serious glances.

"So are we," Janelle answered for both of them.

Christy was thinking about how there are different kinds of hurts and not just the ones that are obvious to everyone else. She knew something about such hidden hurts and the kind of scars friends can leave on your heart.

After thanking Bob, Marti, and Christy, Janelle followed her mom to their car, a lighthearted bounce returning to her steps. If Janelle was about to get in trouble for what happened, she sure didn't appear worried about it.

Once Janelle and her mom were down the street, Mom invited Bob and Marti to come in. The five of them fit comfortably around the kitchen table as Mom offered everyone coffee.

I can't stand this suspense! Christy thought. *Why doesn't somebody say something?* Her lower lip felt numb, and she realized that for the last two hours she had been chewing on it.

At last Dad said, "Christy, what do you have to say for yourself?"

She wanted to cry but fought back the tears. "I'm really sorry. I know we should never have left the hotel room. It was really dumb, and I should've talked my friends out of it."

All four of them were looking at her. She wished she could jump into a time machine and go back 24 hours. She would do everything differently.

"Personally, I think Brittany was the one at fault here," Marti interjected. "She's wrapped up in a whole world of problems, and she pulled the other two right down with her. I'm so relieved that she'll be getting the help she needs."

"This was a raw deal any way you look at it," Bob said. "I was proud of Christy. The police really shook her up, but she showed me that her heart was in the right place."

"Yeah, but her brain wasn't in the right place," David announced from the hallway.

"David! Go outside. Right now," Dad said.

David hurried out the door, and Christy avoided looking at him. For the next 15 minutes, the adults discussed the series of events. Christy felt like a spectator as they evaluated her life.

Once all the facts were clearly laid out, Christy's mom turned to her and said, "Tell us what you learned."

"I learned I have to say no," Christy answered quickly. "And I have to choose my friends more carefully." It felt strange to have all of them looking at her so intently.

A comforting smile pressed across Bob's tanned face. "I know a few 40-year-olds who haven't learned that yet. I'd say the weekend wasn't a total loss."

"I also learned," Christy added, "that no matter what happens to me, the Lord always goes before me and He's always with me." She felt a little bolder than usual, a little surer that her summer promise to Jesus was real and lasting.

No one said anything.

Didn't they agree with her? Did her parents and aunt and uncle understand? It seemed so clear to her.

"Nevertheless," her dad began, sitting up straight in his chair, "there are consequences. You will not be allowed to go anywhere except school for the next two weeks. No social activities of any sort. Do you understand?"

Christy nodded, swallowing hard. She had expected it to be much worse. In an unspoken way, she knew her parents were on her side in this whole thing.

When she wrote about the weekend in her diary that night, she penned:

> The only thing that's going to be hard is not going to church and seeing Rick. I never see him at school. That afternoon at the pizza place was the best time I've had since we moved here. Rick's probably already forgotten about it. He'll probably have another girlfriend by the time I get off restriction.
>
> Why do guys do that? They act all interested in you, and then they forget about you as soon as you're out of their sight.
>
> Like Todd. I'll never forget Todd. Ever. But I bet if he saw me

right now, he wouldn't even remember my name. If only guys weren't
so strange. If only they . . .

Christy stopped writing. She had written herself right into the
middle of the Land of If Only. She knew if she stayed there tonight, she would only get depressed.

Putting away her diary, Christy wrote a short note to Tracy.

I can't tell you how much that verse helped me. It came at a time
I needed it more than I even knew. Thanks so much for thinking of
me and for taking the time to write.

She licked the envelope, sealed it, then pulled out a belated
birthday card for Paula. She had bought it in the hotel gift shop
that morning while Uncle Bob was checking them out of the
hotel. It seemed perfect for Paula. The card said on the front,
"Something has come between us," and inside, "A few thousand
miles! Hope you had a nice birthday at your end of the world."

Christy wrote Paula a little bit about what had been going on
but not many of the details. She wasn't sure Paula would understand, since Christy had been the one who accused Paula of hanging out with the wrong kinds of friends when they were in Paula's
bedroom. If Christy told Paula everything that happened this
weekend, Paula would have every right to give Christy's own lec-
ture back to her. Her closing paragraph to Paula was,

I can't wait for you to come see me next summer. We are going to
have the best time ever. I really miss you. You do know that you're
the best friend I've ever had, don't you? Please always remember that.
Even though things have changed since I moved, I want you to always
know how glad I am that God gave me a best friend like you.

Love,
Christy

The last person she wrote was Alissa. For some reason she felt freer to tell Alissa about all the trouble she had gotten into in Palm Springs. She also told Alissa about the Bible verse Tracy had written in the card to her and how reading that little bit of God's Word had comforted her when she needed it most. Then she wrote:

> You asked why I would make such a big deal about promising my life to Jesus if He were dead like Buddha or Mohammed. The thing is, Jesus isn't dead! Yes, He died on the cross, but then He came back to life and He's still alive today. I can't explain it, but He's living inside me. He's as real as any person I know. I don't know Him as well as I want to, but we're getting better acquainted. I've always prayed—you know, talked to God. But now I'm starting to read my Bible, which is like listening to Him.
>
> Maybe you could find a Bible and start reading it or find a good church you could go to there in Boston. I'll start praying that you'll meet some other Christians who are strong like Todd was and that they'll be able to explain all this to you.
>
> Love,
> Christy

Setting all her letters on the floor beside her bed, Christy slipped under the cool, crisp sheets. She propped her knees up and balanced Pooh bear. She felt clean and fresh and invigorated, as though everything were in order. She was ready for a fresh start at school tomorrow.

"Okay, Pooh. Repeat after me. No, no, no, no! When in doubt, chicken out. No, no, no, no . . ."

The next morning Janelle caught up with Christy in the hall. Janelle's dark, tousled hair looked like a garland of wild black orchids around her head.

"Guess what!" she squealed breathlessly. "Greg asked me to homecoming Friday night! Can you believe it? And I didn't even get to try out my plan to get him to go with me."

"That's great! But what was your big plan, anyhow?" Christy remembered how Janelle's plan had included Rick, and for some reason, that still captured her curiosity.

Janelle didn't answer. Her dark eyes had taken on an exotic glaze, indicating that her mind had flown to parts unknown. Christy knew she wouldn't be back for days.

After school Christy flipped through her locker combination and began yanking her books out when someone tapped her on the shoulder. She spun around and accidentally knocked into the person, spilling her books all over the floor.

"Oops! Sorry!" Christy said before she saw who it was. She stood eye level with the shoulder of a blue and gold letterman's jacket. Her gaze shot up to the guy's face and looked into the chocolate brown eyes that could only belong to Rick.

"Hi!" she said with a giggle. "Did I hit you? I didn't mean to . . . I mean, I didn't see you. . . ."

"You ever consider going out for track?" Rick teased. "You could throw a mean discus."

Christy blushed.

"Here," Rick said, scooping up her books and handing them to her with a smile. "Looks as though you've got a busy week ahead of you."

"Not exactly," Christy said.

"You just like to look smart, right?"

Christy felt as though she were blushing on top of the first blush. Her cheeks must have looked candy apple red.

"Are you going to take time out from all your studies to go to homecoming on Friday?" Rick asked, leaning his arm casually against her locker.

Christy lowered her eyes. "No, I'm not going." She hoped he

wouldn't ask why. It would be so embarrassing to admit that she was on restriction.

"Not even going to the game to see us trample Vista High?" Christy looked up hesitantly and shook her head.

"How about this," Rick suggested in his deep, strong voice. "How about if I pick you up after the game and take you to the homecoming dance?"

Christy's clear blue-green eyes opened wide in disbelief. *He's actually asking me out! What should I say?*

"Rick . . ." Christy tried to find the words. "I would really, really like to go out with you. But you see . . ." She took a quick breath. "Well, I'm not allowed to date until I'm 16."

Immediately, panic seized her. *Will he think I'm a baby? Did I ruin everything by telling him that?* She looked down at the books in her hands and then slowly back up at him.

Rick didn't move. The corners of his mouth were pressed into a warm grin. "Maybe that's one of the things that intrigue me about you so much."

Christy's eyes opened wider as she gazed at him more intently.

"It's your honesty. I think the most beautiful girls are the most innocent ones."

Christy couldn't believe her ears. Her heart raced. *This is the kind of thing a girl dreams of having a guy say to her! Did he really mean it?*

"So," Rick said, pulling his arm back and shifting his books to his other hand, "when's your birthday?"

Christy laughed. "Not until July. July 27th."

"That's only—what?—eight, nine months away? For a girl like you, I could wait that long."

Christy didn't know what to say. She wanted to throw her arms around him and hug him. She wanted to tell him that was the most wonderful thing anyone had ever said to her, that she thought he was the most fantastic guy on the face of the earth. But absolutely no words came out of her mouth. She wished something bright and clever would pop into her mind, but all she could do was smile and swallow hard and smile some more.

"You going to church Sunday?" Rick asked.

"Yes," Christy said, finding her voice. "My whole family is. My dad said this morning that he thought it was time we found a good church, and I told him how much I liked yours."

"Good. Well, I have to go. I'll see you Sunday, if not before."

"Okay. Bye!"

Rick smiled over his shoulder as he started to leave. Suddenly, he turned and said, "By the way, can I call you sometime?"

"Sure!"

"You're not too young to accept phone calls?" he teased.

Christy felt the blush returning to her face. No guy had ever made her blush so much.

"No." She laughed along with him

"Good," he said, taking long-legged strides backward. "I got your number off the card from church. I'll call you sometime."

Christy floated home. For the next hour and a half, she relived the conversation over and over in her mind—everything Rick had said, the way he'd said it, how she had reacted.

Janelle had said he was a smooth talker, and boy, was he! Christy thought it was wonderful. Todd would never say those kinds of things to her. Rick had actually asked her out. It was like a dream. Why did she always have to turn red, though? Next time she talked to Rick, she would be more confident—definitely. More outgoing, too.

David came in from riding his bike and looked at Christy as she lounged on the couch, gazing out the front window. "What are you looking at?"

"Nothing."

"What are you doing?"

"Just making a few wishes."

David walked away, shaking his head. The phone rang, and Christy sprang from the couch, but David had already grabbed it.

"Hello?" he said. Then, "Yeah, she's here."

Christy grabbed the phone from him and covering the mouthpiece said, "Who is it, David?"

"I don't know. Some guy."

Christy's heart bounced into her throat as she put the phone to her ear. Very confidently, she said, "Hi, Rick?"

"Rick?" The male voice on the other end responded.

Christy fumbled through her memory to identify the vaguely familiar voice. "Hello?" she said quickly.

"Is Christy there?"

"This is Christy."

"Hey, Christy, how's it going?"

"Todd?" she asked in disbelief.

"Yeah, how's it going?"

"Todd! I can't believe it's you! How are you?" *Oh no! I hope he didn't notice that I called him Rick!*

"Pretty good."

"How did you get this number?"

"I called your uncle."

"Oh. Where are you?"

"Florida. At my mom's."

"What . . . I mean how . . . I mean . . . well, it's just that I'm surprised to hear from you because you never wrote or anything." The instant she said it, she regretted it.

"Yeah, well, I'm not much of a writer. Not like you. Your letters are incredible. I feel I'm right there talking with you. So, what's been happening? I haven't heard from you in a while."

Christy felt herself relaxing and visiting comfortably with Todd the way they'd talked long hours on the beach last summer. She gave him a quick summary of the disastrous weekend.

He listened intently and said, "Friends can either lift you up or really drag you down."

"I sure learned that," she said. "I've made some big decisions about taking a stand and saying no to people and things that are bad influences on me." She thought Todd would be proud of her decision.

"Sounds cool."

There was a tiny pause, and then Todd said, "Have you started saying yes yet?"

"Yes? Yes to what?"

"Yes to the Lord."

Sometimes Todd's way of thinking was not exactly Christy's way of thinking. "I'm not sure I know what you mean," she said cautiously. She hated to sound dense around him, but she loved hearing his thoughts.

"When I first became a Christian, I was saying no to everything: No to drugs, parties, my old friends, everything. Pretty soon, I was a total loner. I felt as though I were the strangest creature on the face of the earth."

"You? I can't believe that," Christy said.

"Well, then I figured out I needed to start saying yes to something. I mean, no is a good place to start, but being empty is no way to live. So, I started saying yes to God's way of doing things. That's when I found out that His way of doing things is usually the opposite of my way of doing things.

"Anyway, I made a bunch of good friends who were full-on Christians, and before I knew it, instead of all the empty holes from what I'd said no to, my life became really full of all the stuff Jesus was teaching me to say yes to."

"I see," Christy said, trying to understand what he was saying.

Todd probably read her confusion, because he added one of his famous stories. "It's like that boat ride to Hawaii I told you about, remember?"

"Of course I do. I'll never forget that!"

"Okay, let's say you're on the boat. It's this awesome cruise ship with everything you need already on board. I didn't say everything you want, but everything you need. So, you get on board with all these heavy suitcases and bags of junk that you lived off back on shore. You with me?"

"Go on."

"You try to get into your assigned room, but you can't get through the door because your arms are too full. So you go on deck and watch everybody else swim and eat and have fun, but you're hating life because you've got your arms full of all the old junk and you can't do a thing.

"That's when you say no. No to the old stuff you're still carrying around. You dump all that garbage overboard. You see what I'm saying?"

"Yes, I do."

"But then you can't just stand there and keep saying no when the good stuff comes. Like if they ask if you want to eat at the captain's table or play volleyball, you don't keep saying no to everything just to be safe. You've got to learn to make good choices and say yes to the new stuff that God brings to you.

"You see what I mean? There's stuff you have to say no to, but that's only a tiny part of it—the first step, really. If you want to enjoy the cruise, you have to start saying yes. Yes to reading your Bible and going to church and getting close to some strong Christian friends."

Christy took his words to heart. "Todd, I don't know how you come up with these great illustrations, but I love them. You've helped me understand Christianity and what it really means more than anyone else. I really like your stories."

"Yeah, well, I figure Jesus liked stories, too. He told a lot of stories. Have you read the book of John yet?"

"No." The awful truth was, she hadn't read much from the Bible he had given her at all. But she planned to start reading a little bit every day, and she'd decided that even before he called.

"I like John. It's one of the Gospels, you know. And it's full of great stories that Jesus told."

"I'll start reading it tonight," Christy promised.

There was an awkward pause. Christy scrambled for another topic. She loved listening to Todd, and she didn't want him to hang up. Not yet!

"You haven't told me what's new with you," she said. "How's everything in Florida?"

"Oh yeah," Todd said, "The reason I called was to tell you my mom's getting married again."

Christy didn't know how to respond. "Really?"

"Their wedding is in December, and they're moving to New York."

"You're moving to New York?"

"Not me. My mom and her boyfriend. I'm moving back with my dad. To Newport Beach."

"You're kidding!" Christy practically screamed into the phone. "When?"

"Christmas vacation."

"Todd, that is so great! I wondered if I'd ever see you again, and here you're moving back to California!"

"Yeah, it's pretty cool. The thing I'm looking forward to the most is going to the beach some winter morning and cooking breakfast. Shawn and I did that a couple of years ago. We burned the eggs, but the bacon turned out pretty good."

"That sounds like fun," Christy said.

"There's nothing like the beach in the winter. I almost like it more than in the summer. In the morning it's totally deserted except for a few hard-core surfers and about a million seagulls."

"Todd, I'm so excited that you're moving back here! I can't wait to see you again."

"Yeah. It'll be good to see you, too. Hey, I have to go. Do me a favor and practice making scrambled eggs, will you?"

"Okay. Why?"

"So that when we have breakfast on the beach, we can have some decent food."

Christy laughed. "Okay. I'll practice every chance I get."

"Good. Oh, and hey, start saying yes to Jesus, too. He's the best friend you'll ever have."

"I know He is. I will. Thanks. Bye, Todd."

"Later, Christy."

She waited until she heard his end of the line click, and the dial tone hum in her ear. Then she hung up and headed straight for her bedroom.

Her pesky little brother stood by the kitchen doorway. "Who was that?"

"That was a wish come true," Christy said. She impulsively grabbed David and planted a big kiss on his cheek.

"Yuck!" David quickly wiped off his cheek and called to their mom, who was cleaning out the refrigerator. "Mom, Christy's kissing me! Tell her to stop it."

Christy laughed and said, "Sorry, David. I couldn't help myself. I'm just so happy."

Mom appeared behind David with a droopy stalk of celery in her hand. "What's the problem here?"

"Nothing," Christy said before dancing off to her room.

"She kissed me!" David said.

"She kissed you?"

"Don't worry," Christy called over her shoulder. "I can almost guarantee you it will never happen again in your lifetime."

As Christy closed her bedroom door, she heard her brother say, "Why is she acting like that?"

Christy didn't wait to hear her mom's explanation. She twirled around twice, before flopping onto her bed, still grinning from ear to ear. Then, scooping up Pooh bear, Christy hugged him tight and laughed out loud.

Todd is moving to California! Rick actually asked me out! This is one of the most amazing days of my life. After this weekend I thought my whole life was falling apart and now look.

She thought of Todd's story about the cruise and about saying no to all the old stuff so you can start saying yes to all the new adventures God has ahead.

Christy tilted her smiling face upward. *You really do go ahead of me, don't you, God? You're working everything out. You promised You would never leave me, and I believe You because You're right here with me, this very minute, aren't You? I know You are. And You will be with me—forever.*

Christy squeezed her eyes shut, and into the sacred silence that filled her room she whispered one quiet word. "Yes!"

Don't Miss These Captivating Stories in
THE SIERRA JENSEN SERIES

Don't Miss These Captivating Stories in
THE CHRISTY MILLER SERIES

#1 • Summer Promise
Christy spends the summer at the beach with her wealthy aunt and uncle. Will she do something she'll later regret?

#2 • A Whisper and a Wish
Christy is convinced that dreams do come true when her family moves to California and the cutest guy in school shows an interest in her.

#3 • Yours Forever
Fifteen-year-old Christy does everything in her power to win Todd's attention.

#4 • Surprise Endings
Christy tries out for cheerleader, learns a classmate is out to get her, and schedules two dates for the same night.

#5 • Island Dreamer
It's an incredible tropical adventure when Christy celebrates her sixteenth birthday on Maui.

#6 • A Heart Full of Hope
A dazzling dream date, a wonderful job, a great car. And lots of freedom! Christy has it all. Or does she?

#7 • True Friends
Christy sets out with the ski club and discovers the group is thinking of doing something more than hitting the slopes.

#8 • Starry Night
Christy is torn between going to the Rose Bowl Parade with her friends or on a surprise vacation with her family.

#9 • Seventeen Wishes
Christy is off to summer camp—as a counselor for a cabin of wild fifth-grade girls.

#10 • A Time to Cherish
A surprise houseboat trip! Her senior year! Lots of friends! Life couldn't be better for Christy until . . .

#11 • Sweet Dreams
Christy's dreams become reality when Todd finally opens his heart to her. But her relationship with her best friend goes downhill fast when Katie starts dating Michael, and Christy has doubts about their relationship.

#12 • A Promise Is Forever
On a European trip with her friends, Christy finds it difficult to keep her mind off Todd. Will God bring them back together?

FOCUS ON THE FAMILY®

*L*IKE THIS BOOK?

Then you'll love *Brio* magazine! Written especially for teen girls, it's packed each month with 32 pages on everything from fiction and faith to fashion, food . . . even guys! Best of all, it's all from a Christian perspective! But don't just take our word for it. Instead, see for yourself by requesting a complimentary copy.

Simply write Focus on the Family, Colorado Springs, CO 80995 (in Canada, write P.O. Box 9800, Stn. Terminal, Vancouver, B.C. V6B 4G3) and mention that you saw this offer in the back of this book. You may also call 1-800-232-6459 (in Canada, call 1-800-661-9800).

You may also visit our Web site (www.family.org) to learn more about the ministry or find out if there is a Focus on the Family office in your country.

Want to become everyone's favorite baby-sitter? Then *The Ultimate Baby-Sitter's Survival Guide* is for you! It's packed with page after page of practical information and ways to stay in control; organize mealtime, bath time and bedtime; and handle emergency situations. It also features an entire section of safe, creative and downright crazy indoor and outdoor activities that will keep kids challenged, entertained and away from the television. Easy-to-read and reference, it's the ideal book for providing the best care to children, earning money and having fun at the same time.

Call Focus on the Family at the number above, or check out your local Christian bookstore.

Focus on the Family is an organization that is dedicated to helping you and your family establish lasting, loving relationships with each other and the Lord. It's why we exist! If we can assist you or your family in any way, please feel free to contact us. We'd love to hear from you!